"Chase? Are you there?"

At the sound of Kate's voice, he looked at the answering machine, frowning.

"Oh, well, it's Kate. Sorry I missed you. It's seven o'clock, and I just made lasagna and a salad and thought you might like to come over for dinner. If you get home and are hungry, come on over. I'll be up late…" Click.

Gritting his teeth, Chase punched the erase button and reset the machine. It was an act. He could tell by the overly cheerful tone of her voice. She thought she could be sweet as sugar, pretend that nothing was wrong, and all their problems would miraculously disappear.

He didn't know what kind of game Kate was playing this time, but he sure as hell wasn't going to play along.

He'd played the sucker once for her. Never again…

of her butt molded within his hands. She'd always been an ag-

PEGGY MORELAND
Seven Year Itch

Silhouette Books

Published by Silhouette Books
America's Publisher of Contemporary Romance

SILHOUETTE BOOKS
®

ISBN-13: 978-0-373-36116-8
ISBN-10:   0-373-36116-5

SEVEN YEAR ITCH

Copyright © 1994 by Peggy Bozeman Morse

Visit Silhouette Books at www.eHarlequin.com

Printed in U.S.A.

PEGGY MORELAND

Peggy Moreland published her first romance with Silhouette Books in 1989 and continues to delight readers with stories set in her home state of Texas. Peggy is a winner of a National Readers' Choice Award, a nominee for a *Romantic Times BOOKreviews* Reviewer's Choice Award and a two-time finalist for a prestigious RITA® Award, and her books frequently appear on the *USA TODAY* and Waldenbooks' bestseller lists. When not writing, Peggy can usually be found outside tending the cattle, goats and other critters on the ranch she shares with her husband. You may write to Peggy at P.O. Box 1099, Florence, TX 76527-1099, or e-mail her at peggy@peggymoreland.com.

This book is dedicated to Diane Satterlee,
Willie Shales, Nancy Berland, Judy Koepsell,
Shari Villani and Debbie Cowan, friends who were
there from the beginning and whose fingerprints
can be found on every page.

One

Seven year itch? Maybe, but if it was, it was her itch, not his, and Chase Morgan wasn't sure he wanted to scratch it.

For more than two hours he'd waited in the hotel's dimly lighted lounge, a long-neck beer his only companion. For him to be alone wasn't unusual. He preferred it that way. Those whom he called friends knew this particular quirk in his personality and accepted it. Those he didn't, weren't given the choice.

Tall palms flanked him on the right, separating the lounge from the hotel lobby. A slight turn of his head and he had a clear shot of the front entrance. The prick of the palms' pronged leaves on his cheek and sleeve was a small irritant when weighed against the advantage of his secluded position. He wanted to *see,* not be seen.

Earlier, when he'd first arrived, business in the lounge had been slow. Now the crowd was picking up. Women in short leather skirts, tight sweaters and three-inch heels lined the bar. Men gathered in loose huddles behind them, shooting the breeze with their buddies while they checked out the evening's opportunities. Like bird dogs who'd picked up a scent, the men were on point. Happy hour was in full swing and the hunt had begun.

The scene at the bar held little interest for Chase. The only action he was interested in was that created by the hotel's revolving door. Each time he heard its gentle swoosh, signaling a new arrival, every muscle in his body tensed in readiness. He waited for one woman and one woman only.

He slipped a hand to the inside pocket of his jacket. The soft rustling of paper assured him her letter was still there. Why now, after all the years of silence? he wondered.

Just as the question formed, the revolving door swooshed again and the glass panels slowly began to turn. A woman stepped through. Chase batted at a particularly annoying leaf as he strained for a better look. Auburn hair swung shoulder length, brushing a mink jacket of the same rich mahogany. She wore the mink with the same disregard she did the faded jeans that hugged her thighs.

Kate. He rubbed a hand across the light stubble of whiskers on his jaw and silently cursed the slight tremble in his fingers. To steady them, he gathered the beer bottle between his hands and watched her cross the lobby to the registration desk. She moved with the grace and assurance of a cosmopolitan woman, so different from the carefree young woman he remembered.

When she reached the desk, she dropped a leather case at her feet. He glanced at the piece of luggage and pursed his lips in a silent, admiring whistle. Quality. Although he hadn't been raised with it, he knew enough now to recognize it.

A slight movement drew his attention to her feet, and he watched as she shifted her weight from one foot to the other. The action drew his gaze higher to the ripple effect created on the seat of her jeans. She'd always had a cute butt, he admitted reluctantly. The years hadn't robbed her of that.

As he continued to watch, she leaned forward to search through the open purse and her hair fell to curtain her face. With an impatient flick of her wrist, she flipped it back over her shoulder, exposing a three-quarter view of her face. The freckles he remembered scattered across her nose were gone. Makeup or lack of sun? He wasn't sure which, but he wished they were still there. Without them, she seemed more mature, more…like a stranger.

A desire to strangle somebody or some*thing* made him curl his fingers tighter around the neck of the beer bottle. The increased pressure threatened to shatter the amber glass as he fought the pull as well as the memories. Seven years was a long time, but not long enough to forget her.

He watched the corners of her mouth lift in a smile as she handed the clerk a credit card. That smile. He remembered it well. He should. It had haunted his dreams for years. How many times had he fallen victim to its charm? Too many to count, he reflected with a frustrated grunt.

He watched the desk clerk fall all over himself in an effort to please her, and couldn't help feeling sorry for the poor sucker. What is it about her smile that gets to people? he wondered irritably. He raised the bottle of beer to his lips and took a swig. He wrinkled his nose as he swirled the now lukewarm liquid in his mouth.

Maybe it's what the smile does to her eyes, he decided. He was too far away to receive the full impact, but it wasn't necessary. A picture of her face formed in his mind, and he focused on her eyes. Huge, bewitching eyes, the color of new spring leaves. He squeezed his own eyes shut and tried not to remember, yet he knew he could never forget. Tiny gold flecks dotted the irises, sparking her eyes with an energy and love for life—until she smiled. Then the golden flecks danced about, casting a spell on the beholder.

A need to close the distance between them surged through him. He wanted to touch her and talk to her, to see if the changes were only external. No, he reminded himself sternly. He'd only come to satisfy his curiosity…not to talk to her.

What does she want from me?

He shoved the bottle away and it skittered across the smooth tabletop, rocking slowly to a stop just short of the edge. A deep ache throbbed in his chest, reminding him of the pain she had caused. Hadn't she hurt him enough the first time? He'd be a fool to trust her again.

But why does she want to see me? And why now? He reached for the letter as if it might offer some clue. Smoothing open the fold against the table, he read it again.

Chase,
I'll be in Dallas on business in January and would like to see you while I'm there. I'm scheduled to arrive on the afternoon of the 5th. How about dinner at 7:00? Contact me at the Anatole Hotel if this time isn't convenient. Looking forward to seeing you again.
Kate.

He curled his fingers around the letter, wadding it into a tight ball between his closed fist. Hell, she made it sound as if it had only been a month since they'd last seen each other instead of years!

He had no intention of meeting her for dinner. In fact, if she hadn't been so explicit about her time of arrival, he wouldn't be sitting here now. Curiosity had gotten the best of him, and he'd come to prove—if only to himself—she no longer held any power over him.

The knot slowly twisting in his stomach and the deep ache in his chest proved otherwise. He was a fool for being here, yet he couldn't bring himself to leave. Something stronger than his memories held him captive in the crowded lounge, his gaze riveted on the woman at the front desk.

"Not Mrs. McGinis. *Ms.* McGinis." Her clipped words to the desk clerk carried across the short distance to jar Chase with their message.

Ms. McGinis? He knew for a fact that was a lie. When money married money, the news invariably made the headlines. He'd read about both the engagement and the wedding in the Dallas paper himself. Mrs. Philip Michels III. He hadn't forgotten…nor would he ever.

But maybe it wasn't a lie. Maybe she had become one of those women libbers who insisted on keeping her maiden name after marriage to maintain her own identity.

Or maybe she was divorced.

He tensed, mentally squelching the flicker of hope that flamed out of nowhere. Ms. or Mrs. didn't matter, he told himself. He had no intention of getting involved with Kate again.

If she's here on business, why the hell does she want to see me? he wondered. Whatever business they'd had together was settled years ago. In a judge's chambers. She hadn't even bothered to appear.

Knowing he'd seen enough, he settled his Stetson on his head and dropped several bills onto the table. With a nod to the bartender, he headed for the revolving doors at the hotel entrance. He needed fresh air. Space. Distance between himself and *Ms.* Kate McGinis.

Waiting was the worst. At least it was to Kate's way of thinking. By seven, her nerves were playing leapfrog beneath her skin and her palms were so damp she was afraid to touch her silk dress for fear of spotting it. For want of something to do, she paced the length of her hotel sitting room, fluffing cushions and checking to see that everything was neat and in place.

The suite's sitting room was small but comfortable, and a fresh floral arrangement of snapdragons, daylilies and baby's breath added a spot of color on the coffee table. Kate was a sucker for flowers. Even poorly arranged ones, she noted grimly as she eyed the arrangement. She glanced at her watch and groaned. Half-past seven. She'd said seven on her note to Chase, hadn't she?

"Of course, you did, you ninny," she told herself. She was a stickler for detail and always had been. To Kate, time was a commodity, and she had always planned hers to receive the absolute most out of every day. Chase was the one who thought time was something to be toyed with. Appointments, he'd always said, were like promises—made to be broken.

Hadn't he broken the ultimate promise, the one a man and woman made to one another, as easily as he would a dental appointment? "And it seems he hasn't changed much," she mumbled irritably.

Setting her jaw, she snatched up the crystal vase, marched to the wet bar and dumped the flowers on the tiled surface. Droplets of water splattered her dress. She ignored the damp circles, but she couldn't ignore the memory broken promises had drawn.

Her marriage to Chase had been a simple ceremony, just the two of them standing before a justice of the peace, but the promises to her had been no less binding. To love, to cherish, till death us do part.

Though her fingers trembled, she picked up a long-stemmed snapdragon and placed it in the vase, then forced herself to pick up another and another, until the arrangement took shape beneath her skilled eye and hand. By the time the last flower was nestled in place, she was calm again—and vowed to remain that way. The anger and the pain belonged in the past and would do nothing to forge a future for her.

But she had her pride. She wouldn't be caught twiddling her thumbs, looking like she had nothing better to do than wait for him to arrive. Not this time. She'd busy herself, fill the time productively. With this in mind, she picked up the newspaper from the bar and sat down on the sofa. She flipped through the pages to the classified section and began to circle notices requesting bids from interior decorators, and contractors she'd need to contact for future business.

In turning the page to the business section, her wrist rolled—accidentally, of course—just enough to reveal the face of her watch. Nine o'clock. Disappointment slackened her grip and the newspaper dropped to her lap. He wasn't coming. Not even Chase would arrive two hours late.

Disappointment and loneliness weren't new emotions for Kate. She'd suffered the maladies quite often over the past few years, but it didn't make the current feeling stealing over her any more appealing.

Not wanting to give in to the mood, she snatched up the

room-service menu and studied it while she picked up the phone. After placing an order, she changed into a nightgown and robe, then returned to the sitting room to wait. She soon became absorbed in a flickering black-and-white drama on television and jumped when a loud knock sounded on the door.

"Come on in," she called as she stretched to shove the newspaper and lists from the coffee table.

"Just put the tray here on the…" The word "table" died on her lips as she turned. A man stood poised in the doorway. Instead of the red uniform she'd expected, she was greeted with a gray down-filled jacket and a black Stetson hat. The hat's brim left the man's face in shadows, but couldn't hide the square set of his jaw…or the chip he still wore on his shoulder. Years folded back in the split second it took to recognize him.

"Chase…" His name came out on a whispered breath.

"Surprised to see me?"

"Yes! I—I mean, no. I mean—" Mentally, she kicked herself. She sounded like a stuttering fool, even to her own ears. But the very sight of him had her heart pounding and the blood racing through her veins.

A thousand times over the years, she'd told herself her feelings for Chase were nothing but the ghost of a memory she clung to. She'd planned this meeting to put the ghost to rest once and for all. Unfortunately she discovered she wanted more than anything to throw herself into his arms, to nestle against the safety and security of his chest. To feel the warmth again.

But his face was a closed mask, his eyes guarded and un-inviting. She wouldn't let him know how glad she was to see him, she couldn't. Drawing deep on an inner strength that had kept her sane during the last hellish months, she chose her words carefully. "I didn't expect you."

"You didn't?" He pushed the door with the heel of his boot, then leaned back against it as he crossed his arms on his chest. "The letter I received said to meet you here tonight."

The icy disdain in his voice confused Kate. Why was he being so rude? *He* was the one who was late.

"But I expected you earlier. When I didn't hear from you, I assumed something came up and you couldn't make it."

"It's a shame you didn't give me that much consideration seven years ago." He pushed away from the door and walked toward Kate, coming to a stop within an arm's length of her. Though his jacket still carried the chill from outside, Kate felt the warmth of his body pulse between them. "Does this mean you've matured? Or have the years cooled your temper?"

His words stung, but before Kate could respond to the verbal slap, a soft knock sounded at the door.

Chase raked Kate with his gaze from the top of her head to the tips of her bare toes. She clutched at the thin fabric at her breasts as his gaze nearly seared the skin beneath. He raised an eyebrow at her and cocked his head toward the door. "Since you'd decided I wasn't coming, did you call a replacement to entertain you tonight?"

That famous Irish temper Kate struggled so hard to control flamed to life.

"No, I did *not* call a replacement!" she replied acidly, insulted by his suggestion. "I called room service. My invitation to you was for dinner, and when it became evident you weren't coming, I ordered room service. Planning to eat *alone!*" she said through clenched teeth.

With a scowl that said he didn't believe her, Chase turned from her and opened the door to a harried bellhop. The hotel employee looked from Chase's dark expression to Kate's mottled face. "Uh, good evening, Miss McGinis," he said nervously, obviously aware of the tension in the room. "Where would you like the tray?"

"Please set it here on the table by the sofa," she said, reaching for her purse.

"I'll take care of it." Chase paid the tab and opened the door for the bellhop before Kate had a chance to argue. When the door closed behind the bellhop, she intended to give Chase Morgan a piece of her mind. She paid her own way now. She didn't need a man taking care of her. But when the door closed, Chase was shrugging off his jacket and tossing it, along with his hat, onto one of the chairs.

"What's for dinner?" he asked as he walked toward the sofa, briskly rubbing his hands together. "I haven't eaten, either, and I'm starved.

What? Kate screamed inwardly. The quick change in his mood was playing havoc with her nerves. But I won't get angry, she silently vowed. Forcing her fingers to relax from the tight fists she held at her sides, she said calmly, "Since I thought you weren't coming, I only ordered dinner for one. A sandwich and milk."

He lifted the dome lid from the tray. "A club sandwich is always too much for one person. But the milk, now that's a problem." He turned and gestured to the cabinet behind Kate. "Does that bar hold anything stronger than milk?"

"Yes." She sank to the sofa, not trusting her knees to support her any longer now that she'd accepted the fact that he was staying. "There's a refrigerator under the bar."

She heard the pop of a beer can opening; then he was back, pulling the coffee table closer as he sat down on the sofa next to her.

He picked up a triangle of sandwich and offered it to her, but she waved it away, sure she'd choke on anything she put in her mouth.

He took a bite of the sandwich, and she watched his jaws work as he chewed. The fact that he could eat while her own stomach was wrenched into knots inflamed her.

"Why didn't you let me know what time to expect you?" she asked, not even attempting to hide the irritation in her voice.

Chase let out a low chuckle as he wiped a dollop of mayonnaise from the corner of his mouth, then looked at Kate with a smile of approval. "Now that's the Kate I remember. Never mincing words, always going straight to the heart of a matter."

He took a maddeningly long swallow of his beer before he answered. "I didn't call because I wasn't planning to come."

Kate bristled at his bluntness.

Chase patted the air in her direction. "Now hear me out before you start balking. You didn't offer any explanation as to why you wanted to see me, and to be honest, I didn't particularly want to see you."

The words hurt more than Kate had expected. But they were honest, and she could deal with honesty. She hoped he could. "Then why are you here?"

She watched him as he slowly wiped his hands on the linen napkin from the tray. Not one muscle on his face moved to hint at what emotion was running through him. He turned his head and looked at her, those clear blue eyes so achingly familiar yet so distant. His cool look bored a hole straight to her soul.

"Curiosity. It killed the cat, and I'm not ready to die just yet. Why'd you write and invite me here, Kate? What is it you want from me?"

Want? She didn't want anything from him, did she? She

found it hard to think with him looking at her that way and with him sitting so close. All she'd wanted was to talk to him, resolve the past, yet she realized her fingers itched to touch him again—his face, his hair, his lips. Even after so many years, she still remembered the way his lips felt against hers, the way his hands would glide possessively up her sides from her waist until his thumbs pressed against the fullness of her breasts. Warmth crept up her neck and flooded her cheeks at the memory. She straightened, making herself focus on the question, not the man.

What did she want? she asked herself. Why was she subjecting herself to so much pain? The answer came quickly. To resolve her past. To obtain an answer to the question that had haunted her for years. Why had he left her? Was it to avoid commitment, the responsibility of a young wife? Or was it simply because he didn't love her? A hundred times she had kicked herself for not tracking him down and insisting he talk to her, just so she'd know the answer to that question.

Well, she was willing to bare her soul to him to free herself of the past. Was he willing to be as open? She searched his face for some kind of emotion. Anger, hurt or just the simple curiosity he'd named. But there was nothing. No clue to the emotions locked inside.

He'd always been good at concealing his feelings. It had taken Kate a long time to understand that. She'd even felt that toward the end he had begun to open up to her, to trust her. But now she was confronted with the mask again.

"I need to know the truth." She heard the tremble in her voice and fought to control it. "Why did you leave me?"

The flicker of surprise in his eyes was there and gone so quickly, Kate would have missed it if she hadn't been watching him so closely. But she had been, and she saw it before he slipped the mask back in place.

"Leave you? I believe you've got that backward. *You* left me."

"I did not!" Moisture burned her eyes as the disappointment and the hurt experienced seven years before surged through her again. She blinked furiously, not wanting him to see how much pain the memories still caused her.

"I stayed in that apartment for four days," she said, struggling to keep the emotion from her voice. "Alone, worrying myself sick, wondering whether you were alive or dead. You told me you were driving down to Mexico to help some friend of yours who was in trouble. You said it would take six hours, eight at the max. You never called. You never came home. And, yes, I left, but only after Daddy came and told me where he'd found you."

"Found me?" Chase laughed bitterly as he leaned back against the sofa, displaying the only real emotion since he'd entered the room. "*Put me* would be a more accurate phrase."

Indignant, Kate straightened, pulling the folds of her robe protectively across her knees. "I hardly think my father would *put* you in a whorehouse in Mexico."

Chase arched one brow at her. "Is that what he told you?"

Not trusting her voice, Kate only nodded.

"Son of a—" He dropped his elbows to his thighs and his forehead to his open palms, digging the heels of his hands against closed eyes. Several moments passed before he spoke again. "No, he didn't put me in a whorehouse in Mexico." He plowed his fingers through his hair as he fell back against the sofa. "He put me in a *jail* in Mexico, then graciously had me transferred to a jail in Brownsboro, Texas, where he filed charges against me for statutory rape of his seventeen-year-old daughter." He cocked his head toward Kate, his eyes cold and unforgiving. "My wife…. To repeat," he said, each word wrapped in a thick layer of steel, "*you* left me, I never left you."

Kate shrank from him, her head moving back and forth in silent denial. That wasn't what happened. Her father wouldn't do that to her or the man she loved. "I don't believe you," she whispered.

Chase stood and shrugged his shoulders, indicating he didn't give a damn whether she believed him or not. He crossed to the chair and picked up his coat and hat. At the door, he stopped, pushed on his Stetson, then looked back at Kate, his eyes dark and unforgiving. "Ask your old man. See for yourself who's telling the truth."

Two

Kate sat at the scarred wooden desk in the basement of the Dallas County courthouse, a computer printout clutched in one fist. Her knuckles were white, her eyes unblinking. *Case number 439316. Mary Katherine McGinis versus Chase Walden Morgan. Divorce granted by Judge John Thomas Cordray.* The typed words blurred before her eyes.

No! she screamed silently. *She* hadn't filed for the divorce, *Chase* had. Blinking back tears, she searched the copy further, hoping to discover some discrepancy, anything to prove that what Chase had told her the night before was untrue. But everything matched. Names, dates, places. The only difference in the document recorded at the courthouse and the copy she'd held in her possession for seven years was the name of the person who'd filed.

Fingers trembling, she refolded the computer paper and

dropped her hands to her lap. But how? The papers her father had given her to sign had listed Chase's name as requester. If her father had tricked her into signing bogus papers, then had he lied, too, about Chase's whereabouts during those awful days of worrying? Had he really thrown Chase in jail and charged him with statutory rape?

She dropped her elbows to the tabletop and her forehead to open palms. Though the room she sat in was cool, her hands were slick with perspiration and icy against her hot face. *Chase. Oh, God. What did I do to you?*

She sat there for a long time, her thoughts spiraling yet unfocused. People milled around her, phones rang, elevators clanged open and shushed closed in the distance, but Kate heard nothing except the roar of her own guilt in her ears. What had Chase suffered at her hand?

"Do you need anything else, ma'am?"

Kate lifted her head from her hands and glanced up into the face of the clerk who'd helped her. At his look of concern, she scraped the heels of her hands across her cheeks and smiled weakly as she pushed to her feet. "No, I found the information I needed. Thank you for your help." Gathering her briefcase, she nudged in the chair and headed for the bank of pay phones in the hallway beyond.

Hauling the burdensome Dallas telephone directory to the short shelf beneath the phone deck, she flipped to the *M*s and dragged a finger down the page until she found the name Morgan, Chase. Her fingers shaking, she deposited a quarter and punched in the number. The phone rang four times before a recorded message clicked on. The sound of Chase's deep voice brought a new surge of guilt and an ache of regret so strong it nearly dragged her to her knees. Her throat tightened and tears burned behind closed lids.

At the sound of the beep, she fought for control, not wanting him to hear the tears. "Chase? This is Kate. I—" Her voice cracked, and she pressed trembling fingers to her lips. "I—I'm sorry," she finally managed, then added in a whisper, "So very, very sorry." Slowly, she replaced the receiver, then leaned her head against its cool plastic back and let the tears roll unheeded down her face.

Crying did nothing but give Kate a headache. It surely hadn't absolved her of any of the guilt. But she'd called Chase, letting him know she knew the truth. Beyond the apology she'd offered, there was nothing left for her to say or do…at least where Chase was concerned. But there were still a myriad of problems confronting her, the most pressing of which was to find a place to live.

Six hours later, Kate's feet felt like lead and her calves screamed from walking in high-heeled shoes all day. She trailed the Realtor up the sidewalk of the last house the woman had to show her with the same sense of despondency that had settled over her when she'd inspected the first disappointing house earlier that morning.

"I think you'll like this one, Kate," Mrs. Kimbrough offered as she unlocked the front door. "Although it hasn't officially been offered for lease, I know the owner won't mind me showing it to you." She pushed open the front door.

One step inside, and Kate jerked to a stop. Sawhorses sat propped on paint-spattered tarps in the living room while a six-foot ladder dominated the dining room. Carpentry tools were scattered about while empty paint cans topped a pile of debris in the entryway.

But under the clutter, Kate's decorator's eye saw gold. Hardwood floors peeked from beneath the tarps, and the ladder was perched under an antique chandelier whose prisms danced in sunlight cast through leaded glass windows. Though the house had been recently renovated, the owner had taken great pains to retain the home's charm and sense of time.

"There's a darling little breakfast nook through—"

Ignoring the Realtor, Kate darted past her, scurrying through rooms faster than a mouse seeking cheese in a maze. After a whirlwind tour, she returned to the living room breathless, but with her eyes sparkling with newfound excitement.

"I'll take it." She shrugged her purse off her shoulder and dug until she found her checkbook. "I assume the owner will want a deposit and two month's rent in advance, right?"

"Yes, that's correct," the woman said, naming the exact amount.

Kate propped the checkbook against the wall and began to write. "I'd like to move in as soon as possible," she said, scribbling away. "In fact, Monday would be ideal."

"Well, I don't know…" Mrs. Kimbrough replied.

Kate's hand froze and she glanced back over her shoulder. Now that she'd found the house, she couldn't bear to stay in a hotel room any longer than necessary. "Is there a problem?"

The woman's face softened at Kate's panic-stricken expression. "I'm sure Monday will be fine, but I do need to get the owner's approval. He'll want to check references."

Kate heaved a sigh of relief as she turned to complete the check. "You scared me there for a minute. But don't worry. I've got references and a letter of credit from my bank in my purse."

She tore off the check and handed it and the other documents to the Realtor. Another glance around the room and she turned a hopeful look to Mrs. Kimbrough. "Would it be okay if I stayed to work out furniture placement?"

The woman glanced nervously at her watch. "Well, I don't know. I have another appointment at—"

"Oh, you don't need to stay with me," Kate said quickly, to reassure her. "And I promise to lock up when I leave."

"Well…"

Kate heard the waver of hesitation in the woman's voice. "Please?" she added, to sway the scales in her favor.

The older woman eyed her a moment, then smiled. "Oh, I guess so. Just check all the locks before you leave."

As soon as the door closed behind the Realtor, Kate kicked off her heels and danced a jig around the empty living room. After several dizzying spins, she skidded to a stop, pressing her hands to her cheeks to still the whirling sensation. She laughed out loud at the absurdity of her pleasure's source. For heaven's sake, this wasn't her first home! She'd had a gorgeous home in Washington, infinitely larger and finer than the one she stood in now. And before that, she had lived in a darling little garage apartment with Chase.

Chase. Though she'd succeeded all day in suppressing thoughts of him and the past they'd shared, once the memory had formed, she found it impossible to push back. Hugging her arms at her waist, she crossed to a window that opened to the side yard and stared blindly at the house next door.

She and Chase hadn't had much in the way of possessions, nor the time to accumulate any. But what they'd had, they'd been proud of. Three rooms, really, were all the efficiency had consisted of. A bathroom, a tiny galley-style kitchen, and a living room with a three-quarter wall that separated it from the sleeping area. The bricks on the house blurred as Kate smiled through tears brimming in her eyes. Life had been so simple then, so happy.

Rubbing the heels of her hands beneath her eyes, she turned from the window and the memories of Chase and her past to face the room again…her future.

As far as days went, this hadn't been the best. Chase kicked the back door shut, flicked on the light switch and neatly circumvented a pile of paint cans and several cases of ceramic tile. He headed for the breakfast bar, a thin line of tension running from shoulder to shoulder. He despised red tape, zoning commissions and anything that had to do with the government. Unfortunately, for the time being at least, those three things were necessary evils he had to deal with to accomplish his own goals.

The red light of his answering machine blinked at him as he shrugged out of his jacket. He punched the playback button, tossed the jacket across the tiled countertop and picked up his mail, all in one smooth move.

"Chase?"

At the sound of the recorded feminine voice, he jerked his head toward the answering machine. His hands stilled on the stack of mail he was thumbing through.

"This is Kate. I—" A moment of silence filled with nothing but background noise hummed through the recorder; then her voice came again. "I—I'm sorry. So very, very sorry." The last part was so low, Chase had to strain to hear her words. Dropping the mail to the countertop, he hit the rewind button.

"Chase? This is Kate. I—I—I'm sorry." At the sound of

regret in her voice, fingers of steel closed around his heart and squeezed. He strained to place the sounds in the background, wondering if she were still staying at the hotel, and finally decided she must have called from a public phone, probably on her way out of town. "So very, very sorry." He heard the tears, though he knew Kate well enough to know that she was fighting them.

"Damn!" He hit the rewind button and played the message again. And again. By the fifth time, his teeth were clamped together tighter than the iron claws of a trap around a rabbit's foot.

As her voice died away, he closed his hands around the edge of the tiled countertop and dropped his head between his arms. *Damn her!* he railed inwardly. Damn her for not believing in him! Damn her for leaving him! Damn her for showing up again!

And damn her for offering an apology.

An apology, for Christ's sake! As if those simple words could take away the hurt, the empty years, the sense of abandonment. He tucked his forehead into the crook of his elbow and pressed, squeezing his eyes shut until he pushed back the compassion her voice had drawn and let the anger burn through.

No, if she thought a simple apology could make everything right again, she was wrong. Dead wrong.

If she'd had the time to fret about the fact that she hadn't heard from Chase, Kate would have. But as it was, she was so busy, she didn't have time—or so she told herself. A list always helped. A long list, filled with To Do's that kept her hopping from dawn until dusk.

There simply wasn't time to think about Chase. At least, not until the lights went out at night. Then he was there, pushing at her thoughts, keeping her awake, her eyes wide, her heart thumping and the covers twisted around her body from all the tossing and turning she was doing, while she wondered if she'd ever see or hear from him again.

By the day the moving van was to arrive, Kate was exhausted. Dark circles lay beneath her eyes and a worry wrinkle plowed her forehead. Pushing herself, she supervised the unloading of all her belongings.

Once the movers left, she set about putting her house in order. When the last picture was hung, weariness propelled her to the sofa. She collapsed full-length, an arm thrown wearily across her eyes, and slept like the dead. No dreams to haunt her, no voices calling from the past. Just blessed sleep.

Sunlight awakened her. The heat of it boring through the picture window above her warmed her cheek, and she nestled deeper into the cushion, clinging to sleep.

But the sunbeams tickling her eyelashes wouldn't allow it. She lifted an arm laden with fatigue to lay across her forehead and blinked open her eyes. Sunlight bathed the room, capturing the hidden color in the crystal candlesticks on the coffee table, warming the jade vases on the mantel and deepening the jewel tones of the upholstered chairs she'd artfully arranged opposite the sofa. All her things were in place. She was home.

As the thought settled, her gaze drifted to the coffee table. On its polished surface, a wooden, heart-shaped bowl lay between the crystal candlesticks just out of reach. Carved from a chunk of pine, the bowl might have seemed out of place to some, surrounded as it was with crystal and fine porcelain pieces, but for Kate its value exceeded the sum total of everything else in the room.

As she stared at it, tears brimmed in her eyes and the ache

of loneliness settled deep in her chest. Chase had given her the bowl. He'd carved it from a fallen tree outside their apartment. She remembered him laughing as he'd handed it to her, saying he was giving her his heart. Other than her clothes, the bowl was the only thing she'd taken from their apartment. She'd kept it with her, near her throughout the past seven years.

Frustration wove its way through the loneliness. She wanted to see Chase, talk to him. She wanted to know what had happened seven years ago, how it all had affected him. She wanted to know if through it all he'd known she'd loved him.

Fighting back the emotions that pulled at her, she sat up, digging the heels of her hands against her eyes, then scraping them back to hold her hair away from her face. She wouldn't think about Chase. She couldn't. Whatever contact they had in the future would be up to him.

But she had a sister, she reminded herself as she kicked free of the afghan. She didn't have to feel lonely. A simple invitation to Becca and her husband Dan for dinner would solve that particular problem easily enough.

Reggae music pulsed from the CD player concealed behind the wide doors of an antique wardrobe. Sixteen-inch tapers, a deep teal in color, awaited only the touch of a match to bring them to life. The linen spread beneath the candles was of Irish quality, and the china and crystal were Kate's very best. She stepped back from the table to admire her work. Nobody loved to set a mood more than Kate.

Moving her hips to the music's beat, she danced and swayed her way back to the kitchen. Steam rose from gumbo bubbling on the stove top, its scent mingling with that of the sourdough bread baking in the oven. Breathing deeply of the tangy fragrances, she lifted the knife to finish cutting the vegetables for the salad. The kitchen suddenly blinked into darkness, and her throat closed around the indrawn breath.

Momentarily disoriented by the sudden loss of light, Kate dropped the knife and grabbed for the tile countertop and listened. The reggae music was gone, swallowed by the darkness, and only silence hummed through the house.

Her mind searched for an explanation. Had she paid her electrical deposit? A citywide blackout? Not wanting to give life to the thought that came next, Kate felt along the countertop for the knife. Her fingers closed over the wooden handle and she inched her way along the counter until she could peer out the kitchen window.

Beyond the stretch of concrete drive, a streetlight peeked through the naked branches of the oak trees that separated her house from the next. On a closer look, she saw that a light shone from behind the closed drapes of the house next door. Not a blackout, then, and she knew for a fact she'd paid the electrical deposit.

That only left... Don't be ridiculous, she told herself with a shake. There was an explanation for the power outage. The house was old, after all. She felt along the tiles for the phone. Whipping open the drawer beneath it, she pulled out a penlight and her address book. She found Mrs. Kimbrough's number and quickly punched it in.

It seemed an eternity before there was an answer. Kate sagged against the counter, comforted in the darkness by the sound of the woman's voice. "Mrs. Kimbrough, this is Kate McGinis. I'm sorry to bother you at home, but I have a problem. My electricity's off, and I'm expecting dinner guests within the hour."

"Don't ever hesitate to call, Kate, that's what I'm here for. And don't worry about a thing. I'll have someone right over to take care of it."

Knowing help was on its way did a lot toward settling Kate's nerves. She felt her way to the dining room, found the drawer to the buffet and dug out candles. She lit the first one, sunk it into a silver candelabra and let out a deep sigh as its warm glow pushed back some of the darkness. Tucking the other candles under her arm, she headed back to the kitchen using the candelabra to light her way.

Within minutes, candles filled every available space in the kitchen. Some fat and squatty, some tall and slender, with holders varying from fine crystal to dime-store junk, they filled the room with their soft, flickering light.

With a worried glance at the oven and the bread she prayed would continue to bake in the heat trapped there, Kate picked up the knife and began to slice zucchini. A knock at the back door had her dropping the knife in relief.

"Come on in. It's open," she called as she caught up a towel to dry her hands. The door opened, letting in a gust of cold air before closing again.

"Don't you lock your doors?"

Kate whipped her head around at the sound of the familiar, deep voice. *Chase.* A smile bloomed on her face, then froze there.

After a full week of wanting nothing more than to see him and talk to him, she suddenly found herself tongue-tied when confronted face-to-face. Self-consciously, she balled the towel in her hands. "No, I never lock my doors."

"Should. Never know who might decide to walk in."

"How did you know where to find me?"

"Mrs. K. told me."

Her smile fading, Kate watched him move to the plate of switches by the back door. "Mrs. K.?" she asked.

He flipped each one, watching for a response, then moved to the stove and switched on a burner. "Mrs. Kimbrough."

"You're the repairman she sent over?" she asked, her forehead wrinkling as she tried to deal with the disappointment that he hadn't come on his own.

His back to her, he lifted a shoulder in a shrug as he flicked the switch to the off position. "I guess you could say that." He turned and nearly bumped into her. They both grabbed at each other to prevent the collision, her for his chest, him for her elbows. Heat passed from her palms to his chest while the feel of his hands on her bare skin sent goose bumps dancing up her arm. She looked up at the exact moment he looked down. Their eyes met and locked.

He hadn't wanted to come, he reminded himself as he stared into the depths of her green eyes. He'd been certain he could make the call, fix her damn electrical problem and be gone before he did anything foolish or regrettable. But the candlelight was doing things to her auburn hair, plucking out strands of gold while turning other strands to fire.

Acting on instinct alone, he moved his hands from her elbows to the sides of her face and combed her hair back, his fingers tangling in the auburn thickness. Her lips parted, moist and expectant. The desire to pull her into his arms and taste her again flamed, making his hands tighten in her hair. Her sudden intake of breath at the unexpected pressure snapped him back to reality. Quickly, he dropped his hands and stuffed them into his back pockets. He shifted his gaze away from her to glance around the room. "What's with all the candles?"

Kate's shoulders drooped and her hands fell to her sides

as he turned away. She wasn't disappointed, she told herself. No, she wouldn't allow herself to be. "I was in the middle of cooking dinner when the electricity went off."

"Oh." He glanced at the vegetables heaped on the cutting board behind her, then lifted his nose to sniff the air. Kate had never been much of a cook, but she'd tried like hell to please him while they'd been married by trying recipes for everything he liked. Most of it, as he recalled, had turned out burned or tasteless. Judging by the scents filling the room now, her culinary talents had improved dramatically. "Homemade bread?"

"I hope," she said, and slipped past him, careful not to touch him again. She opened the oven door a crack and peeked inside. Heat warmed her cheeks, and she kept her face there a moment longer than necessary so she could blame the heat for the sudden rise in her color. With a quick glance to assure herself that the bread hadn't sunk to the bottom of the pan, she eased the door closed. Not ready to face Chase again quite yet, she picked up the wooden spoon to give the gumbo on the stove top a stir. "Will it take long to repair the electrical problem?"

"Don't know. I'll have to see what's wrong first." And he wouldn't know that until he looked, but at the moment he couldn't tear his gaze away from Kate. The sight of her standing before a stove did things to his heart he didn't want to consider, and stirred memories he'd rather forget.

He watched the sureness with which she stirred and noticed that her hand's churning motion created a similar movement on the seat of her slacks. Muscles tightened, relaxed and tightened again in a rolling motion that drew another memory, one of Kate moving above him, her body slick with perspiration, the cheeks of her butt molded within his hands. She'd always been an aggressive lover, open and giving. His hands itched to touch her and he curled them in his pockets to squelch the notion that was quickly threatening action…one he knew he'd regret.

Not trusting himself to stay in the same room with her, Chase headed for the laundry room, rubbing his hands down his jeans to ease the itch. "I'll check the fuses in the electrical box first," he mumbled as he passed by her.

When she heard the box's metal door squeak open, Kate let the spoon drop against the side of the pan and tried hard not to cry. For a moment she'd thought his appearance in her kitchen meant that he'd come to see her. She almost laughed at the ridiculousness of that assumption as she moved back to the sink. And why would Chase Morgan want to see her? He'd been thrown in jail by her father, charged with statutory rape, deserted by his wife, then served with divorce papers without ever even being asked for an explanation. No, she could certainly understand if he decided he never wanted to see her again.

Using more energy than required for the job, she stuffed vegetable cuttings into the garbage disposal. Intent upon her work, she didn't know Chase had entered the kitchen until he spoke.

"The electricity's back on. Just blew a fuse. I'll turn the lights on for you, then I'll be going."

Kate lifted her gaze to meet his reflection in the kitchen window. He stood tall behind her, his shoulders square and proud, his thumbs hooked through the belt loops of his jeans. His mouth was twisted on one side, as if he were annoyed. With her or with himself? she wondered. Gradually his reflection blurred as tears filled her eyes. She rested her wrists against the sides of the sink, desperately trying to come up with words adequate to express her feelings of regret. "Chase, I—"

Then he was behind her, the weight of his hands at her waist and the warmth of his breath against her neck.

He nudged her hair aside and pressed his lips against the creamy skin of her neck. "Don't, Kate."

She nodded, not trusting her voice to speak. He leaned into her, his groin pressing against her buttocks, his muscled thighs pinning her between the cabinet and the length of his body. Her fingers tightened convulsively on the edge of the sink. Her heart beat like a wild bass drum, and she couldn't seem to get enough air in her lungs. *Does he know what he's doing to me?* she wondered desperately as her body unwillingly responded to his closeness.

Wanting to feel his arms around her, she twisted until her breasts met the warmth and comfort of his chest and her hands the padded muscles on his back. Sharp needles of desire pricked her lower abdomen as he leaned into her, his arms enveloping her in an embrace she'd yearned for.

"Chase, I—" The doorbell rang, interrupting Kate and freezing Chase's fingers at her shoulders.

"Are you expecting someone?" he asked.

"Yes. My sister and her husband are coming for dinner." Leaning back, she looked up at him. "Why don't you stay and join us?"

Chase glanced down at his paint-stained jeans, his scuffed boots, then up at Kate, his gaze lingering on the silk pants and blouse she wore. The contrast was almost amusing. Almost. "No." He stepped away from her, picked up his jacket from the edge of the counter and shrugged it on. "Maybe another time." He pulled open the back door and stepped out, slamming it shut behind him.

Kate listened to the sound of his boots scuffing down the

drive until the sound disappeared. Pride was something Chase had always had a generous serving of, and it appeared he still carried it in the form of a chip on his shoulder.

Sighing, she went to the front door to welcome Dan and Becca to her new home.

Three

Chase settled his fingers around the sledgehammer's smooth, wooden handle, poised its head on the floor with the skill a golfer would use on a nine iron and eyed the wall in front of him. Though he'd planned to spend the evening re-caulking the tile in the master bath, his visit with Kate had left him with a little too much pent-up energy for such a painstaking job.

Taking careful aim, he reared back, lifting the hammer to almost shoulder level, then rolled his wrists and pivoted his body to put all his weight behind the swing. The hammer sliced through the air and hit the kitchen wall with an arm-jarring crack, leaving a hole the size of a chipped dinner plate and spitting chunks of gypsum to the floor.

"Damn Kate McGinis," he swore under his breath as he jimmied the hammer from the wall. Seeing her, touching her again, had left him tense and wanting. Her invitation to join her and her guests for dinner had been tempting... His common sense was all that had saved him from accepting.

Although Kate's father had always deemed the difference in their ages as his reason in keeping Kate and Chase apart, the man had never fooled Chase for a minute. Money was where Chase had come up short in the McGinises's eyes and though he had come a long way in closing that gap, he was still miles from success. At the moment everything he owned—and some he didn't—was tied up in a historical preservation project he was masterminding and a subdivision he and his friend Joe Langford were developing, which when considered, placed him right back in the position he was in seven years ago. Broke.

He raised the hammer for a second swing. "And damn her rich and interfering father," he added as he let the hammer fly.

Clouds of dust puffed from the hole. Already feeling better, Chase pulled the hammer from the debris.

"Hey! Is it safe to enter?"

Chase wiped at the sweat beading his brow as he turned. His partner stood in the kitchen doorway, his hands propped on his hips. Though Chase had thought he wanted to be alone, the sight of his friend made him realize otherwise. "Just tearing out a wall. Come on in."

Joe stepped over the pile of paint cans littering the kitchen floor, shaking his head. "How can you stand to live in this construction zone?"

"Used to it, I guess." Chase braced his hands on the hammer's handle. "What brings you to the slums?"

Joe laughed. "Slums, hell. In the last five years, you've turned this neighborhood into the hottest area on this side of town. Keep this up and Rhonda's going to start badgering me to move again, or at the least, remodel." He eyed the hole in the wall with an exaggerated shudder before he turned for the refrigerator. "Either way sounds like work to me. I thought you weren't going to start on the kitchen for another month?"

Chase turned to pluck a loose piece of wallboard from the wall. "Changed my mind."

Joe popped the top on a beer while he nudged the refrigerator door closed with an elbow.

"Help yourself," Chase said, biting back a smile. Joe's ability to make himself at home with whomever and wherever was one of the reasons they were friends. The fact that Joe put up with Chase's unsociable nature was probably the only reason they remained that way.

Joe grinned and lifted the can in a toast. "Don't mind if I do." He took a sip and let out a contented sigh. "Heard you leased the house over on Kenwood."

"Mrs. K. did."

"So she said. Wise move the day we hired her on."

"She earns her keep."

"She also said the woman who leased it is an interior decorator."

"That's right."

Joe dragged a crate over, upended it and sat down. "I was thinking maybe we might talk to her, see if she'd want to work for us."

Though the idea had also occurred to Chase, it had been a fleeting one, one he'd dismissed as quickly as it had occurred. "I don't think so."

"Look, Chase, I know you like to keep a tight rein on things to hold down expenses, but with everything else going on, I don't have time to spend making all the interior selections. Hell, I'm no good at that kind of stuff."

"We can make do."

"Sure, but wouldn't it be better to make an impression?" Joe's fingers formed a thoughtful triangle around the can. "I was thinking, if we could get her to agree, she could completely furnish a couple of the houses, kind of like they do for the Parade of Homes. It would draw a lot of publicity for us, as well as for her."

Chase frowned, torn between the good sense behind Joe's suggestion and the insanity of getting involved with Kate again. "I don't know," he said hesitantly.

"What's the problem? We need the help. Mrs. K. says the woman's as sharp as a tack."

Chase turned his back on Joe and busied his hands by prying a loose chunk of gypsum from the wall. "She's also my ex-wife."

Joe choked on the beer. "She's what?" he sputtered.

"My ex-wife. Her name's Kate McGinis."

"Holy sh—" His hand shaking, Joe lowered the beer to his thigh. "I had no idea you'd been married before."

Chase sighed deeply. "If you can call it that. We only lived together a little over a week and legally married as long it took the divorce papers to go through. It was a long time ago."

"How long?"

"Seven years."

"I remember reading an article in the paper some time ago about her getting divorced again. I think his name was somebody the third."

Chase thought about what Joe had just said. So, she was divorced after all.

"So how did she wind up leasing your house?"

"Fate, I guess," Chase said with a shrug. "I didn't even

know she was planning on moving back here until Mrs. K. brought me the lease agreement. I thought she was just in town on business."

"Does she know you own the house?"

"No. All my lease properties are incorporated under Vision Properties. I'd just as soon she didn't know."

"I get the impression the divorce was anything but amicable."

"Amicable?" Chase chuckled derisively. "Is there such a thing?" He waved away the question. "It doesn't matter, anyway, it was a long time ago."

"Then what's the problem with hiring her?"

"I don't want her around."

"Oh." Joe sat for a moment, deep in thought, then stood, gesturing with the beer can. "Look. You don't have to work with her. I'll do the hiring, show her the ropes, and you can play the part of a silent partner. I was handling all the interior work, anyway. She'll never be the wiser. You won't have to see her and I don't get a headache sifting through paint chips and wallpaper samples."

"You're lazy, Joe."

"Not lazy, I just know how to delegate." Swallowing the last of the beer, Joe crunched the can in his hand and sent it sailing to join the rest of the litter piled in the middle of the kitchen floor. "Well, we don't have to decide right now. Just give it some thought."

Sitting at the breakfast table with her niece perched in a portable high chair in front of her and her twin nephews confined to the guest bathtub with bubbles up to their chins, Kate was beginning to consider herself a first-class fool…and her sister a saint. *What ever made me think I could handle* these guys for a whole weekend? she thought wearily. She scooped up another spoonful of mashed bananas and offered it to the baby. Shouts of laughter and the sound of water splashing came from the rear of the house.

"Brent! Bryan! You guys cut out that splashing. You're supposed to be soaping up!"

Kate's voice—raised to be heard over the splashing sound, the voices of her nephews and the Sesame Street tape blaring from the stereo speakers in the living room—carried beyond her closed doors and locked windows.

Chase heard her screams all the way from the street.

Out for his evening jog, he'd just passed under the fluorescent glow cast by the streetlight when he heard the ruckus coming from Kate's house. He jerked his head in that direction and slowed his pace. Light spilled from the front windows, turning the leaves on the evergreen shrubs in her front flower bed a warm gold.

He hadn't seen or talked to her since he had repaired her electricity two weeks before, but she hadn't been far from his thoughts—most of them directed toward ways to avoid bumping into her. He'd even considered changing the course of his nightly run, but in the end had decided he wouldn't let the fear of running into her alter his life. So far, he'd been lucky.

A voice pitched high in anger rent the normal solitude and quiet of the street. His breath came in quick puffs of mist in the cold night air as he slowed his pace, cutting a glance toward her house. Should he go to the door and make sure she was okay? Nah, he told himself, and kicked up his speed. She was probably having a party or something. He scanned the driveway with a quick, searching glance and found it empty.

Then he heard her yell again. He couldn't make out her

words, but decided he'd heard enough. Without breaking stride, he cut across the frost-laden grass and leapt over the porch steps in one smooth jump. He jabbed at the doorbell, then doubled his fist and pounded on the door.

At the sound of the doorbell, Kate said in disgust, "Oh, good grief, what next?"

The baby clapped her hands in delight at the musical chimes. Pressing her lips together, she blew, sending a shower of mashed bananas over Kate's tired face.

Then the pounding started. Wiping the splatters from her face with the back of her hand, Kate frowned at the baby. "You sit right there and don't you move. Aunt Kate will be right back."

When she reached the entry hall, she peeked through the peephole and saw a man pacing back and forth across the shadowed length of her porch. Not recognizing him, she cautiously flicked on the porch light just as he wheeled back toward the door. *Chase?* she thought in bewilderment as the light exposed his face. What is he doing here? As she turned the knob in her hand, the door flew open, knocking her back several steps. Chase barged in, his shoulders squared and his fists doubled up, ready to fight.

She watched him spin in a circle, his chest heaving in deep, grabbing gasps, his eyes searching...for what? She took a tentative step toward him. "Chase?"

He whirled to face her, his eyes wide and wild-looking. He reached for her hands and squeezed until she winced at the pain. "Are you okay?"

She stepped back and pulled her hands from his, her own eyes growing wide in alarm. Yeah, she was okay, but was he?

He saw her fear and realized he was the cause of it. "I'm sorry. I didn't mean to scare you, but I was jogging and I heard you scream and—" A loud thump from the direction of the breakfast room had Chase pivoting.

"Oh, no," Kate moaned, and took off at a run. Not at all sure what was going on, Chase ran after her. When he reached the doorway, Kate was bending over, picking up a bowl from the floor.

"Lucky for you it landed right side up, little lady," she was saying in a firm voice to the smiling baby in the high chair.

She scooped up a spoonful of the bananas and held it out as she sat down. She glanced up and saw Chase standing in the doorway, his gaze locked on the baby. She shifted her gaze from him to her niece. Eyes the mirror image of her own looked back at her from a face framed with tight auburn curls the same color as her own.

"Is she yours?" he asked in a hoarse whisper.

Kate smiled as she realized the reason for his surprised expression. "Sort of. This is my niece, Becca's daughter." Her smile turned to laughter as she watched his face relax in relief. "Did you think she was mine?"

"She could be. She looks enough like you."

Wiping a smudge of bananas from the baby's face, Kate cooed to her. "I consider that the highest of compliments, especially since I think she's the most beautiful creature in the world. But, no, I'm just playing aunt and giving Becca a break. Everybody's had the chicken pox at her house and she's been housebound for almost two weeks."

Chase hunkered down in front of the high chair, his palms resting on his thighs, his knee brushing Kate's. "How could you scream at such a sweet, innocent child?"

"Aunt Kate! Help! Brent put soap in my eyes!"

"Did not, you little creep!"

Chase spun on the balls of his feet to face the direction of the cries. "Who was that?"

"Those are my nephews. That's who I was screaming at."

Kate jumped up from her chair and pushed the spoon into Chase's hand. "Feed her."

With the spoon dangling from his fingers, helpless, he watched her run down the hallway. "But I don't know how to feed a baby," he called after her.

"Just fill the spoon and stick it in front of her," Kate yelled back to him. "She'll do the rest."

Skeptically, Chase slowly turned to face the baby. "I hope your aunt Kate knows what she's talking about." He dipped the spoon into the bananas and held it out. The baby tucked her chin to her chest, her lips pressed tightly together, and pushed the spoon away with a chubby hand.

He raised a brow in surprise. "Hey, I thought you were supposed to be hungry?" When she continued to stare at him, her eyes narrowed in distrust, he looked at the dollop of mashed bananas on the end of the spoon and grimaced. "You're right, kid, it doesn't look too appetizing." Taking a deep breath, he added, "But looks can be deceiving." He lifted the spoon to his mouth and took a bite. "Umm-umm good," he said, forcing an encouraging smile as the slimy glob slid down his throat. "Now you try some."

He refilled the spoon and held it out again. She hit the spoon and bananas flew, splattering Chase on the cheek. "Cute," he mumbled under his breath as he wiped the bananas from his cheek to his mouth with his index finger. "Man, that's good," he said for her benefit, and forced himself to swallow. He filled the spoon again and started to take a bite, but stopped just short of his open mouth. "I'm sorry," he said, feigning an apologetic look. "Would you like some?"

She leaned forward, her mouth open. Chase plunked the bananas in before she could change her mind. Proud of himself, he grinned.

Without disturbing Chase and her niece, Kate tiptoed into the breakfast room and leaned a shoulder against the doorjamb. A wistful smile spread over her face as she watched the scene before her. The baby gurgled and cooed in contentment as Chase tried to persuade her to take a spoonful of bananas. Unconsciously, he opened his mouth in encouragement each time he leaned forward, offering her the spoon.

Not five minutes ago Kate had thought Chase a madman, bursting in her front door the way he had. Now here he sat placidly feeding bananas to her niece. She couldn't suppress the laugh that bubbled forth.

Chase glanced her way. "What's so funny?"

"You should see your face." Kate walked over and picked up a cloth to dab at a smear. "You've got bananas all over you," she said, chuckling.

"She's one to talk," he said to the baby as he slipped an arm around Kate's waist. "Do you see that dollop of bananas on the end of your aunt Kate's nose?"

Without warning, he spun Kate to his lap and licked at the offensive blob. Laughing, she struggled to push his face away. Not to be evaded so easily, he caught her fingers in his and licked again. The playfulness of the moment reminded Kate of better times, happier times, shared with Chase. As they wrestled, their gazes met, and in his eyes she saw the same memories, the same regret. The laughter that had come so easily, so spontaneously, slowly faded.

Chase watched her lips part as if she might say something, and before he thought better of it, he pulled her close against his chest and closed his mouth over hers. In response, she wound her arms around his neck and molded her body to his.

For Kate, it was like stepping back in time. His taste was the same, the texture of his lips, the possessive way in which they claimed hers, a memory given life. The strength and comfort she found in his arms, she discovered, was what she'd missed all those years and yearned so desperately to know again.

The need, the desire to let the feelings go on, tightened her arms around his neck.

"Aunt Kate, is this your boyfriend?"

Startled, Kate tore her lips from Chase's. "No," she murmured, her face flaming with embarrassment. She struggled to a sitting position to face the two little demons standing in the doorway.

The question had been posed by Brent, the oldest of the two by six minutes, but Bryan now took over the interrogation. "Who is he, then?"

Not knowing how best to explain her relationship with Chase, Kate replied vaguely. "A friend."

"Do you kiss all your friends like that?"

Kate's only defense was offense. She stood, tugging her sweatshirt back into place. "Did you boys mop up the bathroom?"

"Yes, Aunt Kate," they said in unison.

"Then go to your room and pick out a book, and I'll read you a bedtime story as soon as I get the baby's bottle ready."

She turned to Chase with a pleading look. "Would you mind giving her a bottle while I read the boys a story?"

Although he heard Kate's request, Chase simply stared at her, his mind still focused on her answers to the boys' questions. *Friend, huh?* At least now he knew where he stood with her. He shoved his chair back from the high chair. "What are friends for?"

The sarcasm in his reply was difficult to ignore, but at the moment Kate had her hands full with three children and didn't have time to deal with him. Saving her comments for later, she said, "I'll clean her up while you get one of her bottles from the refrigerator."

She turned her attention to her niece. "Come on, Katie," she cooed to the docile child. "Let's see if we can find that pretty face under all the gunk."

"Katie?" Chase asked.

Noting his puzzled expression, Kate smiled proudly. "This is my namesake. She was born with a full head of auburn hair, and when Dad saw her, he said, 'Oh, no, another Katie,' and it stuck."

The mention of her father had a sobering effect on Chase. Kate noted his subdued look as he turned away to fetch the bottle, but chose to ignore it as she had his sarcasm. Once the children were tucked into bed, though, she planned to discover what was behind his moodiness.

After securing the tape on the disposable diaper, she passed the baby to Chase. "Clean and dry. She's all yours. Turn on the television in the living room if you want some company. I'll be back in a minute."

Her minute turned into a half hour. It took three books on the escapades of Bert and Ernie before Kate finally had the twins asleep. She smiled down at their angelic faces and was reminded of something that Becca often said about her children. "They're sweet, all right...when they're asleep."

"How true," she murmured in a weary voice as she tucked the covers around her two nephews.

When she returned to the living room she found Chase stretched out on the sofa, with his sneakered feet hanging over the arm. Baby Katie was asleep on his chest, her thumb in her mouth, her favorite blanket clutched in a chubby little fist. Kate looked at this tender picture and felt a sharp pain twist her heart. If things had worked out differently between her and Chase, this might be their child snuggled against his chest.

But it hadn't, and it wasn't, so you might as well not dwell on ifs, she told herself as she pushed away from the wall.

She reached down and gently unwound Chase's arms from around the sleeping infant. Cradling the child to her breasts, she carried her to the crib in the guest room where the boys slept.

After tucking the baby in and checking on her nephews, she returned to the living room and knelt beside the sofa. Chase, only inches away, slept, his face relaxed and peaceful. Having him there, stretched out on her sofa, somehow felt right to Kate.

Suspecting that he'd leave if she awakened him, Kate chose to let him sleep. Content just to be near him, she leaned against the sofa's cushions and studied him unobserved.

His looks had changed only slightly in the seven years they'd been apart. Tiny crow's-feet fanned from the corners of his eyes, while a deeper crease stretched across his forehead. She wondered about him, about his life, the missing years, and what worries or concerns might have added those creases. She wondered, too, if she might be responsible for any of the marks. Saddened by the fact that she hadn't been there to witness the changes, she lifted a finger to his face.

She traced the curve of his jawline from ear to ear, careful to keep her touch light. He'd always had strong features. Cheekbones carved high, a chin with the slightest hint of a cleft. The years hadn't changed those features, only matured them, making an already handsome face more handsome by degree. The rasp of five o'clock shadow against her fingertips drew another memory, that of him standing at the bathroom sink in their apartment shaving sometimes as often as twice a day just to keep his beard at bay.

Mired in memories, she drifted her finger upward over the swell of cheekbone to feather lightly across his brow. His eyelids, she knew, covered eyes stained a deep, mysterious blue, eyes that when filled with passion, could turn as dark and turbulent as a storm-tossed sea. Unable to resist, she lifted her face to his and placed a kiss on each closed lid.

He sighed in his sleep and shifted slightly, his elbow brushing against her breasts, his breath fanning warm and moist against her cheek. Kate closed her eyes and breathed deeply, savoring his manly scent mixed with the night air that still clung to him.

Fingers trembling, she lowered them to his shoulders. While she'd been reading to the boys, he'd pulled off the thick outer sweatshirt he'd worn when he first arrived, and it lay in a heap on the floor at her knee. Now a thinner fleece shirt covered his chest.

The sleeves had been shorn off, leaving frayed, uneven edges at his shoulders. Her hands glided across the soft fabric to the bare, muscled arms folded across his chest, measuring the strength there, journeying farther still to rest on the back of his hands. The hands beneath hers were well-shaped and strong, yet gentle when he'd handled the baby, she remembered as she thoughtfully traced a callused knuckle.

Smoothing her hands across and down his broad chest, she felt the rhythmic rise and fall of his breathing. At the sawed-off end of his shirt, her fingertips brushed bare flesh. Dark hair trailed down to his navel, twisting into tight spirals before disappearing behind the drawstring of his sweatpants.

Heat flooded Kate, trickling in a dizzying sensation down from her scalp and up from her toes to pool in her lower abdomen. She curled her fingers at his waist, torn between wanting to explore farther and the wisdom in doing such a foolish thing.

Feeling as tempted as a penniless child confronted with a display of candy, she stole a glance at Chase...and found him watching her.

Four

Heat flamed in Kate's cheeks as his eyes bored into hers. Guiltily, she pulled her hands to her lap. Seconds seemed like years as he continued to stare at her, his eyes unreadable, emotionless.

Then he reached for her, slowly pulling her body up the length of him, his shirt bunching beneath her. Flattened against his chest, she felt the rapid throbbing of his heart echo the quickened pounding of her own.

Only inches apart, he raised his hands to frame her face and drew her closer still. The distance narrowed until their breaths tangled and their lips touched, tentatively at first, like new lovers, experimenting, exploring, savoring the feel and taste of the other.

But they weren't new lovers. Chase knew this as well as Kate. Even as their lips touched, the years folded back, connecting them in a way that suspended both time and conflict. He pressed for a deeper kiss, and Kate's lips parted against his on a low, satisfied moan. He slipped his tongue inside, seeking the sweetness and textures he remembered there. His tongue probed and explored until he found hers, then teased until he drew it between his own opened lips, allowing her the opportunity to taste him, as well.

His hands moved up her sides in that all too familiar journey to press against the fullness of her breasts. His touch was so gentle, so much what Kate wanted, needed, that it stabbed like a physical pain through her chest. She arched away from him, peeling her lips from his. Holding herself aloft, with her hands fisted at his shoulders, she flung her head back and struggled to breathe...to find reason and the courage to stop this madness.

She couldn't do this, shouldn't do this, she told herself. Passion was what had ruled their youth, but logic must govern their future.

Lowering her head to rest her forehead against his, she whispered "Chase..." but couldn't find adequate words to explain her hesitancy.

Though he didn't say a word, he cupped her neck in his broad palm and squeezed. His labored breathing at her ear proved he was as aroused as she, yet he moved his hands to her back and began to draw slow, lazy circles. Gradually the tension she'd experienced moments before ebbed, leaving her limp against him.

Shifting, she rested her head on his shoulder and her fingers found their way to his chest. "Chase?" she whispered as she threaded her fingers through the coarse hair there.

"Hmm?" he responded lazily, not wanting to deal with anything heavier than the weight of her body against his.

"We need to talk."

The muscles in his shoulder tensed beneath her cheek. "About what?"

"About what happened seven years ago."

"Not tonight, Kate."

"But, Chase—"

He stretched to place his lips against hers, then rolled to trap her between his body and the back of the sofa. He kept his mouth against hers until her lips grew pliant beneath his and her fingers stopped pushing against his chest and clung instead. Satisfied that he'd silenced her, he cupped the cheeks of her butt in his hands and leaned back to peer at her. A devilish grin quirked one side of his mouth. "Have I ever told you that you have a cute butt?"

Kate narrowed an eye at him. "You're changing the subject."

"No, just redirecting it. And you do have a cute butt." He moved a hand to trace the logo monogrammed over her left breast. "Along with several other notable body parts."

His finger burned like a hot knife as it moved in slow loops and curves across her breast. Kate closed her eyes against the exquisite pleasure spiraling through her, trying to keep her emotions at bay. Once he'd completed the logo's intricate design, he covered it with his mouth, nipping at her fleece-covered nipple.

Such a simple action, really, yet so erotic…so like Chase. Though her body cried out for him, logic told her that this was the easy way out. To fall into bed and become lovers again without ever dealing with the past was a postponement, a complication and certainly not a resolution.

Knowing this, when his hand drifted down her stomach, Kate caught it at her waist, locking her fingers around his wrist. "Chase—"

He lifted his head to meet her gaze. The passion she found flaming in his dark, stormy depths matched that which burned behind her own eyes.

"Not tonight, Kate," he said, his voice low and commanding.

"But we—"

He pressed his lips against hers to silence her again. "Tonight we don't have a past, just a present."

Her gaze locked on his, Kate swallowed back her arguments. Maybe he's right, she conceded. Maybe they did deserve this one night without all the pressure and problems that plagued their past. Before she could acknowledge her agreement, a distant clicking sound wafted in from the entry hall, then the grandfather clock began to strike. Twelve times it chimed. Then silence.

Kate closed her eyes and groaned. "Chase, I've got to go to bed."

"Just tell me where it is," he whispered against her ear, then nibbled at her lobe.

Kate chuckled as she pushed his head away. "No, you don't understand. Those three little darlings in the other room come back to life at 7:00 a.m., and unless I get some rest, I'll never be able to keep up with them tomorrow."

Frustration seeped through Chase. He'd forgotten about her niece and nephews being in the house. Thankfully, Kate hadn't. Shaking his head to clear the image that had already formed of Kate lying naked beneath him in bed, Chase rolled to his feet and scooped his hooded sweatshirt from the floor. Catching her by the hand, he hauled her to her feet, as well. "Come on, Aunt Kate," he said dryly. "The least you can do is walk me to the door."

In the hallway he turned and before he thought better of it, he pulled Kate into his arms, cradling her head against his chest…when what he wanted was to sweep her up and carry her to the bedroom down the hall.

Every muscle in her body relaxed as she melted against him. She lifted her face to his, her lips curving in a smile.

There it was. That smile. Chase watched the golden flecks in her eyes as they began their seductive dance. He felt himself falling deeper and deeper into their depths, sucked in by an enchantment he couldn't name. He wondered if she had any idea what power she held over him and had held since the first day they'd met.

Once, he'd trusted those innocent green eyes, but now he knew better. Abruptly he pulled away. He jerked his hooded sweatshirt over his head, blocking her from view. The fabric slid down his face until their eyes met again as he slowly tugged the sweatshirt to his waist.

In her eyes he thought he saw the same needs, the same doubts that had haunted him since he'd seen her that afternoon at the hotel, but he couldn't be sure. Slow down, man, he warned himself. We aren't the same people we were seven years ago. We both need a chance to get to know each other again. But he also knew if he didn't get out soon, he couldn't be responsible for his actions.

He reached for the door. "I'd better go."

Kate took a step back as it opened. A blast of cold air hit her, sending shivers racing down her spine. Remembering that Chase had been out jogging when he'd first arrived, she called out to him, "Do you want to take my car?"

"No, thanks," he yelled back over his shoulder. "I don't live far." Without breaking stride, he leapt the hedge separating her house from the one next door, running as if the devil himself were chasing him.

* * *

Loud whispers and the rattling of pans drifted down the hallway from the kitchen. Exhausted, Kate turned over and pulled her pillow over her head.

Remembering her three charges, she shoved the pillow to the floor and sat up wide awake. "Oh, no," she moaned as she scooted off her bed. "What are they up to now?" She ran barefoot down the hall and pushed through the swinging door to the kitchen.

Baby Katie was sitting in her high chair happily banging her spoon on the tray. Brent and Bryan were perched on the counter watching Chase expertly flipping pancakes on the griddle.

"What in the world!"

All four heads turned to look at Kate.

"Uh-oh, guys," Chase said in a stage whisper. "We're busted." Grinning, he moved his gaze down Kate's body, arching an eyebrow appreciatively as he took in her tousled hair, her skimpy nightgown and her bare feet. "Good morning."

Although her brain hadn't quite kicked in yet, she was alert enough to mumble an echo to his greeting. "Mornin'."

"Breakfast will be ready in about five minutes, so you better skedaddle back to your room and get some clothes on."

Though his instructions were clear, Kate simply stood, staring at him. When he'd left the night before, he hadn't said a word about coming back today. Or coming back at all, for that matter, which had kept her awake half the night, wondering. And now here he was, standing in her kitchen, tending three children and cooking pancakes as if he did it every morning. And how had he gotten in? Surely the kids wouldn't let him in without asking first. Or would they? she wondered, her eyebrows drawing into a point over her nose as she frowned at her twin nephews.

Chase walked toward her, brandishing the spatula like a weapon. "Lady, I said, skedaddle!" He turned her around and gave her a whack on the behind with the spatula. "Breakfast in five minutes. And don't be late!" he yelled at her back.

Kate returned to her room and threw on clothes, her mind reeling with unanswered questions, the least of which was how Chase Morgan had gotten into her house. She slipped her feet into loafers and made it back to the kitchen just as Chase poured the orange juice.

While Chase carried Baby Katie and the high chair to the breakfast room, Kate picked up the filled glasses and followed him. They all sat down to heaping stacks of pancakes, sausages, orange juice and milk, a meal Kate wasn't sure she could have prepared herself with three children underfoot.

She shook her head as she spread her napkin across her lap. "Chase Morgan, you amaze me."

He paused in the act of tying Baby Katie's bib around her neck to glance over his shoulder at Kate. "In what way?"

"Look at you," she said, gesturing at him with her fork dripping syrup. "Last night you said you didn't even know how to feed a baby and now here you are, cooking, feeding and wiping up as efficiently as any nanny."

Chuckling, he mashed up pancakes smeared with syrup and spooned them into the baby's mouth. "I'm a fast learner."

"Or an angel from heaven. Either way, thanks. I didn't realize how tiring it was to care for three children."

"I thought you might need some help this morning. That's why I'm here. Unfortunately for you, though, my shift is over and yours is just starting." He pushed back his chair and passed the spoon to Kate. "I hate to leave you with the dirty dishes, but I have some work that has to get done today."

Kate fought the sting of disappointment. "You aren't going to eat?"

"I had my breakfast hours ago, but I'll drop by later, if that's okay? I think we have some unfinished business to discuss," he added, looking at her pointedly.

Butterflies took flight in Kate's stomach at the hidden message in his statement. A tremulous smile curved her mouth as she looked up at him. "Yes, I believe we do. And, Chase," she added as she reached out and caught his sleeve, stopping him. "Thanks."

He caught her hand in his and drew her palm to his lips, sending tingles running down her arms and all the way to her toes.

"Anytime." He waved to the kids and backed toward the door. "Y'all behave now and mind your aunt Kate," he instructed in a stern voice.

"Yes, sir, Uncle Chase," the boys chorused.

Kate's eyes widened as the back door slammed behind Chase. Her marriage to Chase Morgan was the family secret, the one subject that no one ever discussed. Unable to believe that Becca would have shared that secret with her young sons, she repeated in dismay, "'Uncle Chase'! Why did you call him Uncle Chase?"

"He told us we could," Bryan replied innocently.

"He *told* you he was your uncle?"

"No, he just said we could call him Uncle Chase."

Kate dropped her forehead to her open palm, shaking her head back and forth, as if that simple motion alone could free her mind of all the confusion.

With the boys' help after breakfast, Kate cleared away the dishes and began gathering and packing all the paraphernalia the children had brought with them. Just as she put the baby in her crib for a nap, the phone rang.

"Want me to get it?" Brent yelled.

Kate tore down the hall, trying to get to the phone before it woke the baby. "No, sweetheart, I'll get it," she called as she picked up the receiver. "Hello?" she said breathlessly just as Brent pushed through the kitchen door behind her.

"Hi, Kate. Mrs. Kimbrough. Hope I'm not catching you at a bad time."

Kate laughed at the look of disappointment on Brent's face and stooped to rumple his hair. "No, I just put my niece down for a nap and was running a foot race with my nephew."

"Sounds like you have your hands full. I'll only keep you a minute. I heard about a job opportunity and thought I'd pass it along. Mor-Lang Properties is opening a new subdivision and they're looking for someone to handle all the interior selections of the model homes. They are even talking about fully decorating several of the models. Since it would be a chance for you to get your name before the public, I thought you might be interested."

Interested! Kate could barely contain her excitement as she fished in the drawer for a pen and paper. The jobs she'd landed thus far were small. A big project like this could very well double her current client list, while offering a steady income at the same time. "Of course, I'm interested! Who do I need to contact?"

"Joe Langford at Mor-Lang Properties. I'll tell him to expect a call from you."

"Joe Langford at Mor-Lang Properties," Kate repeated as she scribbled the name down. "Thanks, Mrs. Kimbrough. You're a doll!"

Kate replaced the receiver, caught up Brent and twirled him around the room, laughing.

Bryan trailed their steps, tugging at the hem of her shirt. "Dance with me, too, Aunt Kate."

Kate whirled to a stop and set Brent down so she could gather both boys up in a monster hug. "I'll dance your toes off, but first we need to celebrate. Wait right here." She stood and ran to the dining room, returning with the stems of three champagne glasses looped through her fingers. Opening the refrigerator, she pulled out a pitcher of juice and poured some into each glass.

After settling each of the boys on a bar stool with a glass, she propped her elbows on the counter opposite them and held her glass aloft. "Here's to your aunt Kate and—" frowning, she tugged the notepad across the counter "—Mor-Lang Properties," she read aloud. Smiling at the boys, she leaned to tap her glass against each of theirs. "May our business together be a giant step toward a new future for your aunt Kate."

After checking the drive to make sure her car was there, Chase lifted a hand to the door and knocked again. When he still didn't get an answer, he tried the door. The knob turned in his hand.

"The woman has got to learn to lock her doors," he mumbled under his breath as he crossed the threshold. Late-afternoon shadows draped the entry hall and the house was as quiet as a tomb. Either the kids were gone or Kate had managed to get them all down for a nap. Chase was hoping the former was true. This time when he and Kate talked, he wanted no distractions.

"Kate," he called softly, not wanting to wake anyone. He

poked his head around the living room doorway and saw a slender, bare foot peeking from beneath an afghan.

Biting back a smile, he tiptoed into the room, carefully navigating the piles of books and magazines scattered across the floor, and made his way to the sofa. She lay on her stomach, auburn hair fanned across a cushion and draping one cheek, an afghan twisted around her body. The fingers of one hand peeked from beneath the corner of the afghan to brush the carpet.

"Kate?" he whispered. When she didn't move, he eased closer and almost stepped on a champagne glass lying on the carpet, just out of Kate's reach. Was she asleep or had she passed out? Frowning, he squatted down to pick up the glass.

He raised it to his nose and sniffed. Apple juice? Wrinkling his nose, he chuckled softly as he set the glass on the coffee table. As he withdrew his hand, his gaze settled on the crudely carved heart-shaped bowl sitting between the pair of crystal candlesticks. A lump formed in his throat, making swallowing almost impossible.

He reached for the bowl, his fingers settling over the rim of the familiar wood. Taking it in his hands, he dropped down in a chair opposite the sofa. He smoothed a hand over the pine, feeling the grain and remembering. The fallen tree, their garage apartment, the hours of carving with Kate snuggled at his side, watching.

All those years, and still she kept it. Why? He glanced at where she slept. Only half of her face was exposed and even that was partially covered by hair. Last night when things had gotten pretty hot between them, she'd said they needed to talk, and with that, at least, he could agree. He had a few questions himself he'd like to hear the answers to.

He hadn't had a good night's sleep since the day she'd

arrived in Dallas. Each time he'd seen her, he'd sworn to himself it would be the last, but something kept drawing him back. It was time to put it all to rest.

As he watched, her eyelids fluttered. Lazily, like a cat waking from a nap, she stretched, rolling to her side and stretching her arms above her head and her toes to the end of the sofa. Her eyes opened and slowly focused on his face. A slow smile budded on her lips. "You came back."

"Told you I would."

She pushed to an elbow, rubbing the sleep from her eyes. "What time is it?"

"Almost six."

"Six!" Kate fell back with a groan. "I was just going to close my eyes for a minute after Becca picked up the kids, and I slept almost three hours."

"Babysitting's hard work."

"You're telling me." Chuckling, she pulled her hair back from her face and rolled her head to look at Chase. Her gaze drifted to the bowl he held and then back to his face, her smile melting away.

Feeling as if he'd invaded her privacy by seeing the bowl, much less touching it, he leaned forward and set it back down on the table. "Surprised you still have it."

Kate slowly sat up and dragged the bowl from the table to her lap. When she looked up at him, nostalgia had turned her sleep-filled eyes warm. "Do you remember when you carved it for me?"

"Yes."

"And what you said when you gave it to me?"

A longer pause as he shifted in the chair. "Vaguely."

"You said you were giving me your heart." She traced the

rim of the bowl with a fingertip. "Besides my clothes, this was all I took with me when I left."

Chase hadn't known that, and the knowledge both touched him and shamed him in a way nothing else could. "Not much else to take, was there?" He glanced around the room, giving everything a cursory glance. "Looks like you made out better on your second divorce."

Kate, too, glanced around the room. Not one item in it—other than the wooden bowl she held in her hands—had ever graced the home she'd shared with Philip. But Chase didn't need to know that. She set the bowl back on the table and met his gaze squarely. "I did all right."

She stood and unwound the afghan from her legs. "Can I get you something to drink?" she asked as she folded it and draped it over the hook of the sofa.

"I'll take a beer, if you have it."

"You're in luck. I do. I'll be right back."

Chase watched her leave the room, her bare feet padding across the hardwood floors, floors that he himself had stripped and varnished, restoring them to their original beauty. He couldn't help wondering what she would think if she knew he'd done the renovations to this house…and what she'd say when she found out he was the owner.

He templed his fingers in front of his lips and blew out a long breath. A talk was what she'd wanted, and a talk was what she was going to get. But once all the questions were answered, then what?

Before he could turn that problem over in his head, she was back and handing him a frosted mug of beer.

Chase accepted the beer and gestured with it toward the champagne glass sitting on the table. "Been celebrating?"

Seeing the empty glass, Kate laughed. "In a way. I got an offer on a job earlier today, and the boys and I decided to toast the event with apple juice."

"Sounds like you're planning on making Dallas your home."

Kate sat down on the sofa and pulled her feet underneath her, sipping at her iced tea. "If I can build up my business enough to support me, I am."

"Things have been slow here, but the economy's coming back. You should do all right."

Kate looked at Chase, a smile chipping at one corner of her mouth. "Well, we've discussed money. That just leaves religion and sex. Since we never had a problem with religion, shall we discuss sex?"

Chase's brows shot straight up. He snorted, then shook his head, chuckling. "You always were direct."

"One of my many virtues."

"As I recall, we never had a problem with sex, either."

Kate acknowledged the statement with a slight nod of her head. "True. Then what was our problem?"

Kate had always been blunt and comfortable discussing even the most intimate of topics. Chase wasn't and never had been. He shrugged and stared into his beer. "Family might be an issue worth pursuing."

Kate thought about that for a moment, her lips puckered thoughtfully. "Maybe, but my family couldn't stop me from marrying you. That was a decision I made on my own the night I eloped with you."

Chase lifted his head and leveled his gaze on her. "They sure as hell kept you from *staying* married."

"In retrospect, I agree, but initially, I thought my father was rescuing me."

Chase slammed the mug to the coffee table and rose, nailing Kate to the sofa with his gaze. "Rescuing you?" He raked his fingers through his hair as he spun away from her and paced across the room. Wheeling, he faced her again. "From what? Poverty?"

Her eyes on him, Kate slowly released her pent-up breath. "So we're back to the money issue."

"That *was* the problem, wasn't it? Your family had it and I didn't."

"No, money wasn't the problem. At least, it wasn't for me." Calmly, Kate sat her glass of iced tea next to his beer mug and rose, as well. "I left with my father because I didn't know what else to do. You had been gone four days, Chase. For a seventeen-year-old girl—and, yes, I was still a girl— that was scary as hell. And yes, I went home with my father, but not to leave you." She stopped in front of him and reached out to place a hand on his arm. "Only to wait for you to come home for me."

The expression on her face, the tone of her voice, the gentle touch of her hand on his arm all displayed a calmness, an openness that defied Chase's understanding, for he was anything but calm. He'd never been comfortable sharing his thoughts and emotions with anyone. Kate was the only person he'd ever trusted enough to bare himself in such a way, and she'd let him down. Money might have been a part of the issue, but to him, trust played in there pretty heavily, as well.

But damn it, why did she keep looking at him that way, her eyes all soft and warm, so...so accepting and yet so expectant? What did she want from him?

He didn't know and at the moment, didn't care. To hell with trust and whatever else stood between them, all he wanted to do was hold her. His need for her was one thing seven years and Jack McGinis hadn't been able to take away.

Even though he knew doing so was crazy and only asking for trouble, he opened his arms. Kate stepped into them, burying her face in the curve of his neck as her arms circled his waist.

The fragrance, the texture of her hair against his cheek, brought memories humming back that collected in a knot in his chest. He closed his eyes against the ache and tightened his arms around her, gathering her close, setting an anchor in something substantial between them, something that time and conflict had not destroyed.

His need for her.

The doorbell rang, and Chase tensed at the unexpected noise, ready to release Kate, but she ignored the intrusion and, instead, lifted her face to his. "I'm not expecting anyone, are you?" she asked, her lips curved seductively.

Laughter rumbled through Chase's chest as he watched the flecks of gold dance in her eyes. "No," he said, then lowered his mouth to hers. Their lips met, and Kate's breath seeped away, stolen by Chase.

To be in his arms again was like coming home. The comfort, the warmth, burrowed deep inside her, filling her in a way that she hadn't experienced in all the years she'd been with Philip.

"Katherine Michels!"

The explosive sound of her married name reverberated at Kate and she struggled to mentally shove it away, sure that the mere thought of Philip had produced it. The slam of the front door made her realize she hadn't.

"What is the meaning of this?"

Kate twisted in Chase's arms to find Philip standing in the

archway to the living room. Her eyes widened as she sucked in a shocked breath.

"Philip! What are you doing here?"

"I came to see my wife." He shifted his gaze from Kate to Chase. "And who, might I ask, are you?"

Kate took a step away from Chase, but kept one hand clamped tight at his waist. The other she placed protectively at his chest. "This is Chase Morgan. Chase, this is my *ex*-husband, Philip Michels."

Philip crossed the room until he stood almost toe-to-toe with the two of them. He looked down Chase's length, his expression showing his distaste. "So this is Chase Morgan," he said, his voice filled with an arrogance Kate had grown to despise over the years.

Chase didn't like the man's attitude any more than Kate did, but courtesy made him extend his hand. "Obviously, you've heard of me."

Philip eyed the hand a moment before he accepted it. "Yes, I've heard of you." He cut his gaze to Kate. "Although I thought Kate had passed that rebellious stage in her life." He released Chase's hand and turned to shrug off his overcoat and drape it over the back of a chair.

The action was an obvious one of dismissal, and Chase felt the prick of it long after Philip had turned to face them again. Their eyes met and they slowly sized each other up. Chase felt at a disadvantage. Anxious to get back to Kate to finish their discussion, he'd come straight from work at the subdivision, wearing the same sweat-stained shirt, faded jeans and mud-caked boots he'd worked in all day.

In comparison, Philip looked like a paper doll cut straight out of *Gentleman's Quarterly.* Dressed in a navy wool blazer with a cashmere sweater partially concealing his starched pinpoint shirt, a perfect crease ran down the front of his gray wool trousers. He looked exactly like what he was—a slick-tongued, hand-waving politician.

The weight of Kate's hand placed protectively at his chest began to irritate Chase. He didn't need a woman to defend him from the likes of Philip Michels. He peeled her fingers from his chest.

Philip watched the movement, a satisfied smile tipping one corner of his mouth. "Are you leaving?" he asked politely.

"No, he's—"

"Yes," Chase said at the same moment, drawing Kate's surprised gaze to his. He stared at her, trying to shake off the sullied feeling Philip had left him with, but failed miserably. "I'll see you later," he murmured as he dropped his gaze and moved toward the door.

"Chase, wait," Kate called, and started after him.

Philip caught her hand as she charged past him. "Let him go," he said, just as the front door slammed shut.

Kate jerked free of him. "Get out!" she demanded through clenched teeth.

"Now, is that any way to treat your husband?" he chided softly.

"You *aren't* my husband," Kate replied in a tightly controlled voice. "Not anymore."

"Well, that's what I came to talk to you about," he said as he sat down on the sofa, patting the space next to him, indicating for her to join him.

Kate folded her arms tightly across her chest and lifted her chin defiantly. "What do you want, Philip?"

He smiled his most charming smile as he lifted a foot to

prop on her coffee table. "I was in Dallas on business and decided to drop by and see you."

Fired by his boldness, she shoved his foot off her coffee table and flopped down in the chair opposite him. "How did you know where to find me?"

"I telephoned Becca earlier this evening, and she gave me your new address. I thought you'd be staying with your parents."

"I don't need my parents' protection or care. I'm a grown woman and can stand on my own two feet," Kate stated indignantly. Hadn't she proved that to him in Washington when she left him? It just showed how little he knew her.

Her anger built as she watched his gaze move around the room. He glanced at her with a disapproving frown. "Are you leasing this place?"

Insulted by his disparaging tone, Kate lifted her chin. "Yes, I am." Suspicious of his motives for this unexpected visit and anxious to get rid of him, she asked, "Just exactly what do you want, Philip?"

"To be honest, Katherine, I came to take you home."

"Home?" she repeated, her hands tightening convulsively on the arms of the chair. "I *am* home."

Philip stood, moved to stand beside her, and patted her shoulder as if she were a recalcitrant child. "You know very well I mean our home."

Kate brushed his hand off her shoulder. "*We* never had a home. *You* had a home, but it was never mine."

"Katherine, you're a fool." He waved his arm around the room. "How can you possibly want to live in this hovel when you can live with me in my home?" He strode to the fireplace. With his arm resting on the mantel and his foot propped on the hearth, he struck a domineering pose, one Kate was all too familiar with, "The status my name alone offers you is an open invitation to all that Washington society has to offer. Surely you must miss that?"

She missed nothing about Washington, least of all him, and Kate had listened to all she intended to listen to. She clenched her hands at her sides as she rose, that famous Irish temper of hers bubbling to the surface. "How dare you?" She placed her left hand on her hip in a tight fist and pointed the index finger of her right at Philip's chest. "How dare you walk into *my* home and insult me in this way?" She slowly advanced, pointing and pushing until she had Philip backing away. "This house may not appeal to you, but I happen to love it, and I love Dallas and my life here. I will not have you coming here and insulting me or my friends." Philip's backward movement halted when the back of his legs hit the chair. "Furthermore," she continued, "Chase Morgan may not appeal to you, but he does to me. He is a better man than you'll ever be."

At that, Philip's chin came up. Glaring at Kate, he reached over and picked up his overcoat. "You'll rue the day you ever compared me to that ditch digger," he said as he shrugged on his coat. He stepped around Kate and marched angrily from the room, with her following right behind him.

She caught the door as Philip flung it wide, preventing it from banging against the wall, then pushed with the strength of her pent-up anger, slamming it shut behind his back.

She pounded the door with clenched fists. "I hate you, Philip Michels," she screamed. She slid to the floor, opening her hands and dragging her palms down the varnished wood of the door.

With her face buried in the crook of her elbow, she began to sob…not for Philip or the failure of their marriage. She'd dealt with that issue long ago. The hot tears that streaked her cheeks were for Chase, for the lost years, for the injustices he'd suffered as a result of his association with her, and for her inability to spare him from any of it—not from her father seven years ago and not from Philip today.

Five

Clutching the address of the firm in her hand, Kate searched the registry on the wall beside the elevator of the Tyler Corporation building.

"Mor-Lang, Mor-Lang, Mor-Lang," she muttered as she moved her finger down the list.

Oh, Lord, she thought in despair when her finger lit on the name. Twelfth floor. She glanced at her wristwatch. But if luck is with me and the elevator works, I still might make the two o'clock appointment on time.

Never one to be late, Kate blamed her current rushed state on Chase. She'd spent the entire morning pacing, dialing his telephone number and leaving increasingly more anxious messages for him to please call her. All to no avail. He had never answered the phone, nor had he bothered to return one of her calls.

She made the ride to the twelfth floor, her toe tapping impatiently, her fingers thrumming the corner of her leather portfolio. When the doors slid open, she bolted from the elevator and located the office of Joe Langford without a moment to spare. She stopped outside his office long enough to straighten her business suit, catch her breath, gather her wits and push Chase Morgan to the back of her thoughts. This job was important to her, and she couldn't afford to allow thoughts of Chase to distract her from the business at hand.

Tucking her portfolio neatly under her arm, she entered the office and, putting on a confident smile, approached the secretary.

"Hello, I'm Kate McGinis. I have a two o'clock appointment with Mr. Langford."

"Yes, Ms. McGinis. He's expecting you. Please come with me."

Kate followed the secretary into an adjoining office and stopped with a quick intake of breath. "Good heavens!" she gasped, her fingers tightening on her portfolio. The office looked as if it had exploded. Carpeting, tile and brick samples were strewn across the room. Rolls upon rolls of blueprints lay propped against the walls. There wasn't a spot on the floor that wasn't littered. Kate lifted her gaze to the secretary. "Are you sure he's expecting me?"

"I'm sure," the woman said, laughing as she slipped past Kate and closed the door behind her.

Kate heard a muffled oath and looked around in search of the owner of the voice.

She took a cautious step farther into the room. "Mr. Langford? Are you in here?" she asked.

"Kate? Is that you?"

"Yes." She followed the sound of the voice to an open door, then stopped as a huge bear of a man backed out of the storage room, burdened down with wallpaper sample books. Just as he turned to greet her, his foot caught on a stack of bricks and he tripped, crashing to the floor at her feet.

Kate's hand flew to her mouth. "Mr. Langford, are you all right?" she asked as she bent over him.

He started laughing. A big, booming, contagious laugh that had Kate smiling in spite of herself.

"I'm sorry we had to meet like this, Kate, but as you can see, I'm really snowed under in work." He made a huge sweep with his arm indicating the messy room, then slapped his thigh and roared with laughter at his own joke.

Puzzled by his odd behavior, Kate wondered if he'd suffered a blow to his head in the fall and had knocked himself senseless. "Are you sure you're all right?"

"Yes. I'm fine. Even better now that you're here and can take this mess off my hands. I've been telling my partner we needed a professional to handle this decorating business, but he wouldn't listen. Now he's finally come to his senses. And," he added, arching one eyebrow at Kate, "I can certainly see why."

She looked at him in confusion. "I'm sorry, Mr. Langford, but I'm not here at your partner's request. Mrs. Kimbrough suggested I call for an interview."

For a moment the man looked frustrated. "R-r-right," he stammered, and glanced away as he began to shove the wallpaper books away from him. "I'm just glad to get all of this decorating responsibility off my back and out of my office." He stuck out a hand. "Now give me a hand and help me up."

Kate assisted him as he struggled to raise his huge bulk from the rubble scattered around him. Once on his feet, Joe dusted off his slacks, then caught Kate at the elbow in a pawlike hand. "Tell me about yourself," he said as he guided her to his desk.

"Well," Kate began, plucking up a string of Formica samples before sitting down in the chair Joe angled her way. "My business here is less than a month old, but I owned my own business in Washington, D.C." She passed Joe her portfolio. "These are examples of some of my work there."

Joe flipped through the pictures as he eased a hip onto the corner of his desk. "Have you ever done a model home show before?"

"No," Kate answered. "But as you can see," she said, gesturing to the portfolio, "I've overseen the interior selections of several homes from the architect's pen to the laying of the carpet and everything in between."

Joe closed the cover on the portfolio and handed it back to her. Thoughtfully, he crossed his arms at his chest, seemingly satisfied with her answer. "The job we're offering here is pretty flexible. You'll be making the interior selections on all the homes and fully decorating and furnishing three for our grand opening. You have free reign as far as design goes, but you'll be given a budget to work within, and I'll need to approve any overages."

He stretched behind him and picked up a paper from his desk. "We've never used the services of an interior decorator before, but we're hoping you'll find the compensation we've arrived at fair."

He passed the paper to Kate, and she scanned it briefly. A weekly base salary, commissions on the sale of any of the furnishings sold during the grand opening and a bonus when the house itself sold. Considering the amount of publicity she'd

receive and the contacts she'd make as a result of her partici-
pation, Kate viewed the arrangement as more than fair.

Smiling, she handed the contract back to Joe. "I would
request one other thing."

"Oh, and what's that?"

"I'd like to serve as a hostess in one of the houses during
the grand opening."

Grinning, Joe rose and extended a hand. "You've got
yourself a deal."

Kate rose, as well, and shook the offered hand. "Thank you."

"Leave your address and telephone number with my secretary, and I'll have one of my men deliver all this junk to
you tomorrow."

"This is not junk, Mr. Langford," Kate said, feigning an
insulted look as she gestured toward the piles of samples
filling the room. "These are the tools of my trade."

"Yeah, right." He chuckled as he guided her to his office door.
"And, please, the name's Joe. Makes me nervous when people
call me Mr. Langford. I start looking around for my dad."

Every time the phone rang or the doorbell chimed, Kate's
heart leapt, hoping beyond hope that it would be Chase. It
wasn't. Nearly a week had passed without a word from him.
As promised, Joe Langford had delivered all the plans and
samples for the model homes. Kate had buried herself in
sketches, drawings and floor plans in an attempt to block
Chase from her mind, but by Friday morning she was a wreck.

She needed to get out of town, to relax and forget Chase
Morgan. So someone would know her whereabouts, she
decided to check in with her sister before leaving town.

"Becca, it's Kate."

"Hi, sis. How's it going?" Becca piped in a cheerful voice.

"Wonderful and rotten. Business is the wonderful part. Personal is the rotten. I haven't heard from Chase since Philip offended him Sunday night."

"Kate, this is the twentieth century. Pick up the phone and call him. Explain what a pompous ass Philip is. He'll understand."

Kate dug her fingers through her hair. She propped her elbow on the desk and rested her forehead in the palm of her hand. "I did call him. And I've left a hundred messages. He hasn't returned one of them. I even called Mrs. Kimbrough to see if she could get in touch with him for me, but she said he was out of town and wouldn't be back until Monday."

Becca's voice was soothing. "Poor Kate. Don't give up. Monday's just a couple of days away."

"Right. But in the meantime, I'm going crazy. I can't stand being in this house one more minute." Frustrated, she fell back against her chair, dragging the phone to her lap. "I'm going to drive to Canton and go to First Monday. There are some antique pieces I need for a project I'm working on that I can probably find there. Don't worry if you can't reach me this weekend. I may stay over if it proves to be a good sale."

"Mom and Dad returned from Florida last night. Why don't you call and see if Mom wants to go with you? She loves antique shopping as much as you do."

Becca's suggestion was a good one, but considering the awkwardness of her relationship with her parents—specifically her father—Kate decided a personal visit rather than a phone call might prove more productive. If she called and her father happened to answer the phone, she wasn't at all sure he'd allow her to speak to her mother.

With this in mind, she threw a change of clothes and her necessities into an overnight bag, tossed it into the trunk of her car and headed for her parents' home.

When she pulled into the driveway, she drove around to the back and parked her car in front of the garage. Settling back against the seat, she simply looked, letting memories and emotions wash over her.

Though the front of the two-story home Kate had grown up in was formal and projected the image of wealth and success important to her father, the rear of their home painted an entirely different picture. Here her mother's touch was in evidence.

Wisteria clung to lattice panels surrounding a large back porch. Terra-cotta pots of varying shapes and sizes stood empty now, but with the advent of spring would fill the porch and adjoining fan-shaped patio with every flower and color known to man. On the back door hung a wreath of dried flowers and eucalyptus, and at its threshold a Welcome mat. This was the door Kate had used growing up. Coming home from school and bursting inside, knowing her mother would be there to greet her.

Kate closed her eyes and could almost smell the scent of brownies baking in the oven. When she opened them again, moisture clung to her lashes, drawn there by the memories and the confrontation awaiting her.

Ever since she'd told her parents about her plans to divorce Philip, there had been a rift in their relationship. Though her mother—God love her—had tried to remain neutral, her father had refused to speak to her. To spare her mother the emotional strain of being pulled between her loyalties to her husband and her daughter, Kate had elected to stay away. At times, Kate found that separation more painful than another encounter with her father.

Sighing, she stepped from her car and headed for the back door.

"Kate? Is that you?"

Kate turned, throwing up a hand to shield her eyes from the glare of the sun. "Mother?"

"Over here, dear. In the garden."

Kate headed for the white picket fence that surrounded her mother's herb and vegetable garden at the rear of the property. She should have known to check there first. While growing up, Kate and the rest of the clan had always known to look in the garden when they couldn't find their mother.

Unlike most of the women in her social group, Lilah McGinis didn't mind getting her hands dirty. While her friends spent their mornings sprawled on the couches of their analysts, whining about their unfulfilled lives, Lilah happily hummed, dug and planted in her garden. Through the years her garden had given her hours of pleasure, as rich and nurturing as the soil she tilled.

She'd shared that love of nature and the peacefulness it offered with each of her children.

As Kate approached, her mother pushed open the gate, peeling dirt-encrusted gardening gloves from her hands. Kate paused, the months of self-imposed isolation leaving her feeling awkward and unsure of her mother's greeting.

Fighting back tears, Lilah opened her arms and gathered her daughter close.

"Oh, Kate, sweetheart," she said, leaning back and tipping up Kate's chin for a look at her oldest daughter. "You look wonderful."

"Liar," Kate said, laughing, scraping back her own tears. "I look like hell and you know it."

"Tired, is all," her mother soothed, tucking her arm through Kate's. "A nice cup of tea will put the color in your cheeks."

Though the tea and a cozy visit sitting opposite her mother at the kitchen table sounded inviting, Kate hung back. "Is Dad home?"

Her mother stopped and looked back. "Yes."

Kate glanced away and nodded toward the garden. "Why don't you show me what you're planting before we go inside?"

Lilah caught Kate's hand in hers and squeezed in understanding. "I wasn't planting anything. Only playing in the dirt." Keeping Kate close at her side, she strolled to the grape arbor where an ancient glider rested, nestled beneath its arch. "Let's sit here in the sun where it's warmer and you can tell me what's bothering you."

"Who said anything's bothering me?" Kate asked defensively.

"No one, dear," Lilah said, patting the space next to her as she sat down. "Mothers just know these things."

Frowning, Kate flopped down, her abrupt movement setting the iron seat screeching as it shot forward on its rusty base. They sat in silence, the glider gradually settling into a soothing motion beneath them. Lilah waited patiently while Kate twitched and fidgeted next to her.

Finally Kate blurted out, "I've seen Chase." She mentally tensed, waiting for the storm. When it didn't occur, she stole a glance at her mother. "Well? Aren't you going to say anything?"

Lilah just smiled. "When you called and said you were moving back to Texas, I assumed you would see Chase at some point."

"You aren't angry?"

Lilah patted Kate's thigh. "No, dear, I'm not angry, though your father probably will be."

Kate snorted. "Moot point since he hasn't spoken two words to me since the night I told him I was divorcing Philip."

"Give him time. He'll come around."

"In this lifetime?" Knowing her mother didn't deserve the brunt of her anger, Kate sighed. "Did you know that Dad arranged Chase's and my divorce?"

"No, but I suspected as much. How did you find out?"

"Chase told me. But I didn't believe him. I went to the courthouse and pulled the records myself. Even though I know how manipulative and overbearing Dad can be, I still find it hard to accept that he would do such a thing."

Lilah twisted around in the seat, pulling one leg beneath her until she faced Kate. Catching a lock of her daughter's hair, she lifted it away from Kate's face and tucked it behind her ear. "He did it because he loves you."

Tears burned in Kate's eyes as the anger bubbled back. "Loves me? He has an odd way of showing it. Throws my husband in jail, has him arrested and charged with statutory rape, then has bogus divorce papers delivered to me so I'll think Chase is requesting the divorce, not me." Kate balled her hands into tight fists on her knees and glared at a patch of smiling-faced pansies growing alongside the flagstone walk. "If that's love, he could have fooled me."

Lilah chuckled softly.

Kate snapped her head around to frown at her mother. "It's not funny, Mother."

"Yes, it is. You are so much like him. Stubborn, willful and full of passion."

"I'd thank you," Kate replied sarcastically, "but that sounds like a list of vices, not virtues."

"Depends on how those traits are put into action." Knowing she'd said enough about her daughter and husband's relationship, she changed the subject. "How is Chase?"

"Fine, I guess. Or at least he *was* fine." Kate sighed again and dropped an elbow to the glider's arm and her cheek to her palm. "Philip dropped by while Chase was at my house last Sunday. Philip was his usual, obnoxious self. Chase left before I could apologize, and I haven't heard from him since."

"Call him."

Kate cut her gaze to her mother, surprised that she'd suggest such a thing. "I did. He's out of town and won't be back until Monday. In the meantime, I'm going stir crazy."

"Here." Lilah dug in the voluminous pockets of the smock she wore beneath her jacket and pulled out a small trowel. She slapped it into Kate's hand. "Dig in the dirt."

Kate couldn't help but laugh. "Good idea, but I have a better one. I'm going to First Monday in Canton and I thought maybe you'd—"

"Lilah! Where are you?"

Kate jumped up at the sound of her father's roar and dropped the trowel to the ground.

"Over here, dear," Lilah called as she stood. She laced her fingers through Kate's.

"Lilah, I can't find my golf sweater. Have you—" As he rounded the corner by the arbor, his gaze met Kate's. He stopped and stared a full ten seconds, his mouth puckering into a disapproving frown. "Hello, Katie."

"Hi, Dad."

He stared a moment longer, then shifted his gaze to Lilah's. "Have you seen my golf sweater?"

Hope sagged out of Kate. She hadn't seen or talked to her father in over six months and all he had to say to her was, *Hello, Katie?*

As if she sensed her daughter's disappointment, Lilah tightened her grip on Kate's hand. "Yes, dear. It's in the armoire, top left drawer. I'll get it for you. Kate and I were about to have a cup of tea. Why don't you join us?"

He lifted his chin imperiously, his frown deepening. "Have you forgotten? We have a golf game with the Morrisons. Our tee time's at one."

"But Kate's only just—"

Kate stepped between them. "That's okay, Mother. I need to run, anyway."

"But, Kate—"

Kate gave her a quick hug. "Another time. I'll call you when I get back in town."

Her father arched a brow her way, one corner of his mouth twisted into a scowl as she walked toward him.

Though she had tried hard to escape without having words with her father, that last look of his sent her good intentions scurrying for cover. "Oh, and by the way, Dad," she said, smiling sweetly up at him. "I know about your involvement in Chase's and my divorce."

His eyes widened and his face turned a mottled red. Knowing she had the upper hand, Kate went for the kill. She rose on tiptoes to plant an impudent kiss on his cheek. As she lowered her heels to the ground, she rested a hand on his arm. "I know you did it because you love me and wanted only what was best for me. But you were wrong, Dad. Chase Morgan is the best thing that ever happened to me. I loved him then, and I love him now."

I loved him then, and I love him now. I loved him then, and I love him now...love him now...love him now. The phrase picked up the tire's cadence on the road and spun it around and around in Kate's head, nearly driving her mad.

She slapped the heel of her hand against the padded steering wheel. "Why did I say that to Dad?" she asked, glaring at her reflection in the windshield.

Because you still love Chase.

"I don't!" she denied, her fingers tightening on the steering wheel until her knuckles looked like a string of pearls draped there.

Then why did you contact him again?

"Because I wanted to resolve my past. That was the *only* reason."

Tell it to somebody who believes it.

"Uu-ugh!" Kate raged as she pressed the accelerator to the floor, attempting to flee her thoughts of the man who haunted her. Focusing her attention on the road signs whipping past, she watched for the one indicating her turnoff.

Seeing the exit for Canton, Kate turned off I-20, determined to put Chase out of her mind and enjoy herself.

On the weekend before the first Monday of each month—thus its name—people gathered their wares and set up booths in Canton, Texas. It had grown over the years from a small flea market to the almost carnival-like atmosphere Kate now viewed as she parked her car. The booths were filled with everything from puppies to priceless antiques.

No matter what you were looking for, you could always find it at First Monday…and more. The colorful shoppers walking, talking and eating as they meandered through the maze of booths soon had Kate forgetting the problems she'd hoped to leave behind in Dallas.

She spied a Mexican woman selling tamales from the bed of an old pickup truck. She purchased a couple of the spicy Mexican staples and began to walk down the aisles separating the booths, eating hungrily as she looked from left to right, afraid she might miss something.

By late afternoon she was burdened down with purchases: a crib quilt for Baby Katie in a log cabin pattern, hand-carved tops for her nephews, peach preserves for Becca, an old apothecary jar for Dan to add to his collection of pharmaceutical supplies and daffodil bulbs for her mother.

She hitched the bag of purchases higher on her hip. It was definitely time to make a trip to the car to stash her finds. Just as she decided this, she spied a pine cupboard at the end of the row. Her interest drew her on until she reached the piece of antique furniture. Standing back with her head cocked to the side, she appraised the cupboard. It was unpainted and in excellent condition. A visual picture of it sitting in one of the Mor-Lang houses formed. She knew she had to have it.

The dealer was leaning against a table, working a chaw of tobacco around the inside of his jaw and seemingly uninterested in Kate. She approached him, anyway. "Excuse me. How much are you asking for this piece?"

The man slowly straightened. "Well, ma'am," he drawled, pausing to spit a stream of tobacco between his feet. "This here's a fine piece of furniture. It came out of my old granny's house and she was mighty partial to it." He crossed his left arm at his waist, propped his right elbow on it and gazed at the pine cupboard for a moment. "I can remember when I was a kid watchin' her pull out that bottom drawer there and measure out the makings for a pie."

Kate was prepared for this. She had bargained with dealers before and knew hype when she heard it. This man was going to put a high price on this piece, but she loved to bargain.

"I'm sure she made delicious pies. How much did you say you wanted for the cupboard?"

He turned his gaze from the cupboard to Kate. "I didn't." He shook his head in regret. "Granny'll probably turn over in her grave, but I'm willin' to part with it for say…six hundred dollars."

"Six hundred dollars!" Kate echoed in surprise. "That's more than I'd planned to spend," she said apologetically, and turned to walk away.

The dealer quickly moved behind her. "I can see that you're a lady who 'preciates old things. I think Granny'd be proud for you to own this here piece. I'm willing to give it to you for five-fifty," he offered, his chest swelling with pride at his magnanimous offer.

"I'm afraid you're still too rich for my blood." Kate walked to the pine cupboard and rubbed a hand across its work-worn surface.

The dealer walked up beside her and stood there, scratching his head for a minute. "I'd jest hate to see you miss out. Tell you what, you can have it for five hundred, but that's the lowest I'm agoin' to take, and I'll be only be makin' that offer to you."

Kate stepped back and looked the cupboard over again as if unsure of her decision. Though the price was still more than she'd like to pay, she knew the cupboard was well worth it. "I'll take it," she said, reaching out to shake the hand of the dealer.

"You shore made yourself a deal," he said. "Now how you plannin' to get it home?"

Kate looked from the dealer to the cupboard and frowned. It certainly wouldn't fit in her car. Why hadn't she thought of that before? "Do you think I could rent a U-Haul trailer in Canton and come by tomorrow to pick it up?"

"I'll haul it for you, lady, for a price."

The sound of the richly timbered voice behind her made Kate do a double take. Not wanting to hope, but hoping nonetheless, she slowly turned around. "Chase," she murmured, not quite believing her eyes. "Where did you come from?"

He looked behind him and pointed down the narrow walkway crowded with people. Kate couldn't help but laugh. "No, I mean, where have you been?"

He lifted a shoulder and let it drop. "Fishing."

"How did you know where to find me?"

"I didn't, I came here to pick up some lures. But it looks like a good thing I happened along," he said with a nod toward the cupboard.

"Oh, yes. The cupboard." Kate frowned and turned to look at her oversize purchase, then laughed. She moved to slide her arm through Chase's and smiled up at him. "It seems my taste exceeds the size of my trunk. Got any suggestions?"

"I've got a truck," he said helpfully.

"And you don't mind hauling the cupboard to Dallas?" she asked, just to be sure.

"Not unless you need it before Sunday night. I'm not planning on going home until then."

Relieved, Kate said, "No. Sunday will be fine." She turned

to the dealer and made arrangements for Chase to pick up the piece later.

Gathering Kate's smaller purchases under his arm, Chase twined her fingers through his free hand. "Let's see what else you can't live without," he teased.

Kate stole a glance at his profile as she matched her steps to his long stride. I've done everything in my power short of placing a missing person report to locate this guy and darned if he doesn't just show up where I least expect him.

Unable to contain her curiosity any longer, Kate stopped, tugging Chase to a stop, as well. "Did you get my messages?"

His forehead knitted into a frown. "What messages?"

She searched his face, sure that he was playing dumb, but found only innocence. She tightened her fingers in his. "The ones I left on your answering machine."

"No." Sensing her uneasiness, he smiled. "But you can tell me now." He guided her by their clasped hands to a booth selling hot chocolate and purchased two cups filled with the marshmallow-topped cocoa. He nodded in the direction of a cluster of picnic tables. "Let's sit down over there."

They sat on the redwood bench with their backs to the table, their knees only inches apart. Chase leaned back, resting his elbows on the table, steam rising from the cup in his hand, and looked up at the gathering clouds in the sky.

Kate studied his upturned face. Relaxed, rugged, reassuring. Her fingers itched to touch him, to warm her hands on his skin. She clutched her cup with both hands and settled on the warmth it offered instead. She'd waited for days to offer an apology for the way Philip had treated him, but now the words were hard to form. Only the simplest came to mind.

"I'm sorry about Sunday night."

Chase's chin leveled with a jerk and his warm expression faded. "No apology necessary."

"Chase." Kate placed her hand on his thigh and felt his muscles tighten beneath it. "Philip is an arrogant man, at best. At his worst, well… I'm just sorry you felt you couldn't stay. You missed the fireworks."

He arched one eyebrow and cocked his head toward her. "Fireworks?"

"Yes, fireworks," Kate repeated, with the memory of her exchange with Philip bringing anger to her tone. "Philip infuriates me. He's such a snob. The only blue-collar shirt he owns he wears with a gray pin-striped suit. He considers anyone with dirt under their fingernails and calluses on their hands beneath him." The description so well fit Chase's current appearance, Kate jerked her hand from his thigh, clamped her lips together and looked away from his penetrating gaze, sure that in trying to apologize she had only offended him further.

Chase hooked the blunt tip of his index finger under Kate's chin and pulled her face back to his. "How do *you* feel about blue-collar workers, Kate?" he asked softly.

Her eyes pooled. "Oh, Chase. I don't care what you do for a living. I…" She caught herself before revealing a deeper emotion, one she wasn't able to admit to herself yet. "You're a special friend to me and nothing else matters."

Friend again, Chase thought in frustration as he stared into her upturned face. The same description of him she'd fed to her nephews, but after a week spent analyzing their relationship, it was not one Chase was willing to accept. A low rumble of thunder in the distance drew his gaze to the storm clouds scudding across the sky.

"Looks like we're in for a storm. We better head back," Chase stood and drained his cup. "Where are you staying?"

"I'm not. That is," Kate clarified, "I stopped here first, planning to shop before checking into a motel in Canton."

He took her cup from her hand, pushed it into his and threw them both into a paint-chipped litter barrel beside the table. "My cabin's not far. Why don't you have dinner with me, then I'll bring you back to your car?"

She looked at him in surprise. "I didn't know you had a cabin here."

He tucked the sack of purchases under one arm and draped his other one around Kate's shoulder. "There's a lot about me you don't know."

Their hips bumped together as they walked, and Kate enjoyed the sensation. "Okay," she said after a moment, accepting his invitation. "I'll have dinner with you, but only if you let me help cook." She wrapped her arm around his waist and tipped her head back to look up at him. "Seems like I remember you cooked the last time."

Chuckling, Chase led her in the direction of the crowded parking lot, teasing her at all the stops she made along the way. Afraid she'd miss a good purchase, Kate hung back, scanning the booths as Chase urged her along.

"Oh, Chase, look!" She dropped her arm from around his waist as she spied an unfinished pine harvest table with four ladder-back chairs pushed to it. "That would look great with the cupboard I bought." She walked toward it, then stopped and looked back at Chase. He was standing in a slouch where she'd left him, one knee cocked, his hand pushing at the waist of his jeans. His lips were drawn into a scowl.

"If memory serves me right, you already have a breakfast

table *and* a dining room table. What do you need another table for?"

A gust of wind kicked up and blew Kate's hair across her face. She laughed as she finger-combed the hair behind her ear. "It's not for me, silly. It's for one of my clients." She turned, hugging her arms beneath her breasts as she eyed the table. "Don't you think they belong together?"

That's what Chase loved about Kate. Everything took on a new sparkle when seen through her eyes. It had been that way seven years ago when they'd first met and, thank God, she hadn't changed. He moved to stand beside her. "Like a horse and carriage."

But he wasn't looking at the table. His eyes were on Kate.

Six

With the storm clouds gathering quickly now, the owner of the table and chairs settled quickly on a satisfactory price with Kate. An early darkness began to settle over the area and the smell of rain permeated the air.

Chase backed his truck as close to the sales area as possible. With the help of the dealer, they quickly loaded the table and chairs, moved on to load the cupboard, and covered it all with a tarp.

As they pulled onto the highway, Kate settled back against the seat of the truck and pulled her knees to her chin. "Don't you just love the furniture?" she asked, pleased with her purchases.

Chase smiled indulgently at her. "I've yet to meet a woman who didn't get a thrill out of spending money."

She gave his shoulder a playful shove. "Oh, you. I don't enjoy spending money. I just happen to believe I bought two excellent pieces of furniture and saved my client several hundred dollars to boot. And *he,* I'm sure, will be proud of my bargaining talents, even if you aren't," she stated with a lift of her chin.

"Who's 'he'?"

"Mor-Lang Properties."

Chase studied her profile a moment, wondering if she had a clue he owned half of Mor-Lang. The feigned haughtiness told him she didn't. He turned his attention back to the road and hooked his wrist over the top of the steering wheel. A smile tugged at the left corner of his mouth. "Yeah, I'm sure he will."

Rain began to pelt the windshield, forcing Chase to turn on first his windshield wipers, then his headlights. Kate strained forward against her seatbelt, a worried frown on her face. "How much farther is it?" she asked nervously, concerned for the furniture loaded in the back.

"Not far." Chase lifted an index finger and pointed down the road. "About three miles down on the left, there's a farm market road. Two miles farther, on the right, is a rock road that runs across a cattle guard. That's the road to my cabin."

Kate settled back against the seat and watched the rhythmic swish of the wiper blades. She saw the sign for FM-314 just as Chase slowed on the rain-slick road to make the turn. With her forehead pressed against the side window, she watched for the rock road he'd mentioned.

They bumped across the cattle guard, and the tires spun for a second on the loose gravel before connecting and shooting forward. Chase pulled the truck under a shed to protect the furniture from the storm. He turned to Kate with a grin. "This is it. You ready to make a run for it?"

She glanced back through the rear window at the pouring rain and groaned. "Ready as I'll ever be."

Lightning streaked across the darkened sky and, seconds later, thunder rumbled through the towering pines surrounding them. Chase wrapped his arm protectively around her shoulders, and she huddled against his side in the open doorway of the shed. Rain beat against the shed's tin roof, deafening them to any other sound. Chase leaned his mouth close to Kate's ear and shouted, "Run!"

He darted out into the downpour, dragging her at his side. Rain streaked down their faces and within seconds soaked them to the bone as they splashed across the soggy, leaf-strewn ground to the cabin.

Chase shouldered his way through the door and pulled Kate in behind him. Leaving her standing in the doorway, he shook out of his rain-soaked jacket, hung it on a peg by the door and strode to the fireplace.

Kate stood a moment, waiting for her eyes to adjust to the darkness. A match flamed in Chase's hand, then blazed as he touched it to the tinder in the fireplace. She shivered. She was cold...but curious. She'd never been in Chase's home in Dallas and had no idea how he lived. Anxious to catch a glimpse of the private side of his life, she glanced around.

They were in a large room with rough-hewn log walls, four-paned glass windows and a fireplace. Chase knelt on a braided rag rug in front of the fireplace, one hand resting on the hearth while with the other, he worked the buttons on his shirt free from their buttonholes. He shrugged his shoulders back and forth to shuck the sodden fabric from his body and down his arms. Muscles rippled across his back and bunched on his upper arms beneath a layer of bronze skin.

Kate's own skin began to tingle, and a warmth spread from between her thighs and rose to thicken at the back of her throat. She tore her gaze from Chase's naked back to stare at the kitchen on her right.

Forcing her mind to focus on her inspection, she noted pressed-back chairs pushed up to an old oak pedestal table closest to her. Beyond the table, against the back wall, stood a blackened wood-burning stove with a blue granite kettle perched on its grate. Beside the stove, firewood stood in a neat stack. Blue and white gingham curtains hung at the single window above the kitchen sink and there were dishes on the drain board.

Simple, clean and orderly. Much like the man. She glanced at the John Deere calendar tacked on the wall beside the table. December. She smiled. Thank God. I was beginning to think he was perfect. She walked to the calendar and flipped the page to the correct month. February. Next Friday would be Valentine's Day. A day for lovers.

She glanced toward Chase again. What would it be like to be his lover again? Would he be gentle? Considerate? Tender? Or would he be strong, demanding and totally physical? She remembered him as being all those things, but feared time and distance had shaped and shadowed her memories.

He lifted another log, his muscles flexing under the strain, and threw it on the fire. When he leaned forward, his jeans slid lower on his hips, revealing a thin band of paler skin. Kate's breath rattled out of her, while her fingers curled into tight fists.

She watched him rub his hands briskly across his thighs as he stood, brushing off the debris from the logs before turning to look at her. Their eyes met and locked. As if in slow

motion, he moved toward her. He took her hand loosely in his.
"You're cold." Warmth spread up her arm as he tightened his
grip and began to chafe her hand between his.

Rain dripped from her jacket and pooled on the hardwood
floor at her feet. Hooking his thumbs on her jacket's lapels,
Chase pushed it off her shoulders. It slid down her arms and
dropped in a heap in the puddle of water. A shiver shook
Kate's shoulders.

"We need to get you out of these wet clothes." He pulled
her to the crook of his arm and guided her to the fire. "Stay
here by the fire, and I'll see if I can find you something dry
to put on."

Kate sank down on the hearth and watched him disappear
into an adjoining room. Drawers opened and banged shut.
Doors opened with a squeak and slammed closed again. Then
came the sound of running water. Chase reappeared, carrying
a bundle of clothes and wearing a smile.

"I'm not sure these'll fit, but at least they're dry." He pulled
her to her feet, and with the clothes pressed between them, he
touched his lips to her purple ones. "You're freezing," he said in
a hoarse whisper, his fingertips brushing lightly across her cheek.

Kate stared back at him, her eyes wide with wonder at the
tenderness and concern she saw in his eyes. He guided her
toward the door. "Come on. I've run you a warm bath. There
are towels in the chest behind the door. I'll change while
you're bathing, then I'll start dinner. Okay?"

Kate nodded, pressed the bundle of clothes to her breasts,
and backed toward the bedroom door, unable to tear her gaze
from his. Her heel hit the wall first, then her head. Embarrassed by her awkwardness, she spun and hurried through to
the bathroom beyond.

Freezing, she stripped quickly and stepped into the tub. Hot water lapped around her as she inched her body into the old-fashioned footed tub. The chill slowly eased from her body, leaving her warm and lazy.

Sinking down until her head and shoulders were all that protruded from the steaming water, she closed her eyes and listened to the sound of Chase moving about in the other room.

She heard the creak of the bedsprings and the thump of a boot hitting the floor. With her eyes closed, she could imagine him peeling off his wet jeans and briefs and walking barefoot and naked to the chest of drawers in search of dry clothes. The image alone was enough to have her throat closing over an indrawn breath.

Straining to listen, she heard the crackle of starched denim as he pulled on clean jeans and the grate of metal on metal as he snugged up the zipper. The bedsprings creaked again as he sat to tug on his boots, then the sound of his footsteps as he left the bedroom and headed back to the kitchen.

Sighing heavily, Kate relaxed against the chipped porcelain tub and let her mind drift, wondering about Chase and what the future held for them.

Enticing scents wafted under the bathroom door and drew her from the warm cocoon of her bath and her thoughts. Remembering her promise to cook, she forced herself from the tub and dressed quickly. She cuffed the shirt he'd loaned her to her elbows, discarded the oversize jeans and completed her outfit by tugging on a pair of his woolly socks.

When she emerged from the bedroom, she found Chase busy in the kitchen, a dish towel tucked at the waist of his jeans. "Can you really cook on that stove?" she asked doubtfully as she watched him drop something into a large cast-iron pot perched there.

"I manage," he said, a trace of a smile lighting his eyes when he glanced her way.

"Mmm, it smells good. What is it?" Kate asked as she dipped her head over the pot and sniffed.

"My portion of dinner, and you better get busy on yours."

Kate shot the blackened stove a skeptical look. "I'll help, but I've never cooked on a wood-burning stove."

"It's not hard. Here." Chase handed her a large mixing bowl. "You mix up the corn bread batter, and I'll heat up the muffin pans."

Kate was soon busy stirring up the batter while carrying on a lighthearted banter with Chase.

After popping the filled muffin pans into the oven, Chase tugged the dish towel from his waist. "We've got about thirty minutes before the muffins are ready. Let's sit by the fire."

Kate curled up on the couch, and Chase settled down on the rag rug at her feet. He leaned his head back on the cushion beside her, and she couldn't resist combing her fingers through his thick hair.

"Tell me about your work, Kate."

Her fingers stilled, surprised by the question. "There isn't much to tell." Her fingers moved again, massaging at his scalp. "I'm working on several small projects, but my biggest challenge is the job for Mor-Lang." She became totally absorbed in her subject as she told Chase about the new sub-division, sharing her ideas and plans for the houses she was decorating for the corporation's grand opening.

"The pine furniture is for one of the houses I'm decorating as a model. It's a ranch-style house with a large kitchen that opens onto the family room. I'm shooting for a country look and that table and cupboard will be perfect."

"You really enjoy your work, don't you, Kate?"

Her fingers stilled in his hair. "I love it! The constant challenge of a new job and the pride that comes with a finished project. Not to mention the thrill of spending money," she teased as she ruffled his hair. "But I've been talking a mile a minute. What about you? Tell me about your work."

Chase reached his arms up over his head, locked his hands in a tight fist and stretched. "Muffins are about ready. You hungry?" He stood and turned to pull Kate to her feet.

He'd neatly avoided her question. Was it because he was ashamed of what he did for a living? Or was there some other reason behind his reluctance? Considering the fragility of their relationship, she decided to let her question slide for the time being and smiled up at him. "Starving." She wrapped her arm around his lean waist and walked with him to the kitchen.

"You set the table. I'll dish up the stew," Chase instructed as he moved to the stove.

He set bowls of steaming stew on the table, then turned the corn bread muffins onto a platter. After pulling out Kate's chair, he slid onto his own.

Steam rose from the spoonful of hot stew she blew on before tentatively testing the liquid with her tongue. "Chase, this is delicious," she said in surprise. "When did you learn to cook?"

"Necessity is an excellent teacher. Years with only my own cooking to nourish me made me a fast learner. Some of my earlier attempts weren't edible." He lifted his spoon in gesture of a toast. "But I've improved with time and practice."

Eating in companionable silence, Kate emptied her bowl

and pushed it away with a groan. "I'm stuffed. If I hang around you for long, Chase Morgan, I'll be as big as a cow."

Chase grinned. "You ever see a skinny cow that looked good?"

Kate's shoulders sagged as a sense of déjà vu washed over her. She propped her elbow on the table and rested her chin in her open palm. "Do you remember when you took me to the farm to meet your grandmother?"

Chase nodded and took another bite of corn bread.

"She cooked enough to feed an army and kept shoving food at me, telling me to eat up. When I complained that she was going to make me fat, she said almost that exact thing to me." Moisture glistened in Kate's eyes.

Chase half rose from his chair and leaned across the round table, resting his palms on either side of the stew bowl. He planted a kiss on Kate's lips, then leaned back and looked at her upturned face. "Yes, I remember. And I remember my reply. Do you?"

She felt a flush slide up her face and looked down at her empty bowl. She picked up her spoon and swirled it around the dregs in the bottom of the bowl. "Something about your not caring if I was as big as a cow."

"And something more."

Surprised that he'd remembered, Kate glanced up and then quickly down to her bowl again. "You said you didn't care how fat I was as long as you were the only bull allowed in the pasture."

Chase sank back into his chair and tipped it until it balanced on the back two legs, his gaze never leaving Kate's face. "That offer still stands."

Kate wasn't ready for this, yet there was no denying the attraction. It strung between them as tightly as a coiled spring.

But she'd made one mistake on the rebound, she didn't intend to make another. To fall into a sexual relationship with Chase with nothing other than the promise of physical satisfaction would surely be a mistake. She loved him. She'd admitted as much to her father. But did he still love her? Seven years was a long time.

She stood abruptly and pushed back her chair. "I'll do the dishes," she said, and began to busily stack them.

Chase watched her hands as she nervously gathered the plates, bowls and silverware. He rocked the chair down on all four legs with a thud. He'd spent an entire week analyzing his feelings for Kate, trying to decide if they had a chance for a future. He'd finally convinced himself they did, but he'd also promised himself he'd go slow, he wouldn't rush into anything. Yet he'd purposely insinuated an affair. And she'd turned him down flat.

"We need some more firewood." He grabbed his jacket from the peg by the door and left, slamming the door behind him.

Kate moved to the sink and began to fill it with water. Bubbles grew translucent and shimmering in the soapy water. She pricked one with a fork and watched it burst into tiny droplets. Just like her dreams. Seven years ago her dream had been to live out her life as Chase Morgan's wife. Like the bubble, that dream had burst. Kate stirred her index finger through the suds in slow circles.

What did Chase expect of her? What did he want? The more she was around him, the more her need for him grew. Would he ever trust her again? Would he ever be able to share himself with her? He'd avoided her question about his job. If he couldn't talk about something as simple as that, she doubted he'd share anything as private as his thoughts, his needs…his feelings for her.

As she heard his boots scrape on the front porch, she quickly piled the dishes into the sink and began to scrub them with a vengeance, her back to him and the door.

She listened to his movements as he moved across the room behind her, stacking wood and levering more into the fireplace. Yet he never spoke or came near her. That fact alone kept her head down and her own tongue silent.

After she finished cleaning up, she dried her hands, carefully folded the dish towel and placed it beside the sink. Turning, she found Chase stretched out on the sofa.

She tiptoed across the hardwood floor and turned to warm her backside at the fireplace.

"Where do we go from here?"

Thinking he was asleep, she was startled by the question. Nervously, she balled her hands behind her back. "I don't know."

Chase scrunched his shoulders down farther into the cushions, his eyes still closed, and folded his arms across his chest. "We've got to quit pussyfooting around the issues."

Kate stiffened. "I couldn't agree more."

"What do you propose, then?"

She glared at his closed eyes. "You might start by looking at me."

After a moment of stubborn silence, he opened one eye and cocked his head toward her. He stretched his arm out toward her. "Come here."

With an insolent glance at his arm, Kate returned her gaze to his. "*You* come here."

He chuckled, then offered, "Meet you halfway." He rolled to his feet and stood, waiting for Kate to move. When she didn't, he lifted his arm, his hand outstretched, his palm open and waiting between them.

With her eyes narrowed in suspicion, she placed her hand in his. He grasped it and shot her a devilish grin. Before she had a chance to react, he gave her hand a tug and they both fell onto the couch in a tangle of limbs.

Kate twisted free and sat up. "You cheated."

"Did not."

"Yes, you did. You didn't even take a step."

Chase wrapped his arm around her middle and pulled until her face was within inches of his own. "Neither did you."

She opened her mouth to deny it, then clamped it shut. He was right. She hadn't taken a step. "I hate it when you're right."

"I know." Chase tugged on her earlobe with his teeth. "But I usually am."

Kate propped her elbows on his chest, and with a deep sigh, allowed the length of her body to match his. "We really messed things up, didn't we?"

Chase brushed her hair back from her face with a slow finger, knowing she referred to the past. "Yeah, we did."

"Why didn't you ever re-marry?"

"Why *did* you?"

Kate pursed her mouth in a pout. "Do you realize you never answer a question?"

"Don't I?"

She slapped at his chest. "See? You did it again."

"You answer my question, and I'll answer yours."

"Because you dumped me."

Chase opened his mouth to deny it, but she pressed her finger to his lips. "I thought you dumped me." With her elbows still propped on his chest, she picked at the polish on her thumbnail. "After our divorce was final, Dad shipped me off to Washington for the summer and I met Philip. We started dating. I was rather vulnerable at the time, and he made me feel loved."

She felt Chase's body tense beneath her, but refused to let it affect her or her explanation. After all, he'd asked the question.

"What I didn't realize was that I was just another step in his career plan. He needed a wife, and I fit the necessary qualifications. After we married, I realized *feeling* loved wasn't enough. I needed to love and *be* loved. With one failed marriage under my belt, I tried to make it work, but it just wasn't there."

Moisture filled Kate's eyes as she glanced up at Chase. Suddenly she realized why her marriage to Philip hadn't worked. There had never been room in her heart for Philip Michels. Chase had dominated the space. For six years she'd compared Philip to Chase—and Philip had come up lacking every time.

Realizing this, and shamed by it, she hurried to explain. "Please don't think I blame Philip totally, because it was just as much my fault as his."

Chase thumbed a tear from Kate's cheek. "Was it a messy divorce?"

"No, not to the public. I filed for the divorce, and Philip didn't contest it. I guess he feared the bad press if we fought it out in court. He did manage to make my life miserable, though."

"Why?"

"Oh, I don't know. I've tried to figure it out, but the only answer I can come up with is that Philip can't stand to lose, and he lost me. I know it sounds bizarre, but you'd have to know Philip to understand."

It was over. It was the past. And Kate didn't care about Philip anymore, but it didn't stop the hurt. She remembered the whispers behind her back, the cold shoulders received from people she'd once called friends, and the anger at being followed by a private investigator. And now she couldn't stop the tears. They started as a simple burning sensation behind her eyes, a tightening in her throat as she fought to hold them back. Moisture built and pooled in her eyes. Her nostrils flared and burned. Then the dam broke. She buried her face in the crook of Chase's shoulder.

He cradled her head to his chest. "Don't cry, Kate." His lips brushed against the top of her head and he smelled the rain in her hair. He shifted his shoulder until her face was turned to his. His lips touched the corner of her eye, and he tasted the salt of her tears.

"I—I—I'm sor-r-r-ry. I d-d-didn't mean t-t-to cry." A shuddering sigh escaped her. "When I w-was growing up, I h-h-hardly ever cried. Now it seems it's all I ever do."

Kate sat up between Chase's thighs. Using the edge of the borrowed shirt, she wiped her eyes. "Now, tell me why you never re-married."

Chase pushed himself with the palms of his hands to a sitting position, his knees chafing against her hips. He combed her hair back from her face with his fingers. "Because the only girl I ever loved dumped me."

She opened her mouth to deny him, then laughed instead. "Like I said, we really messed things up, didn't we?" He smiled back at her, and she ducked her head as she wound the hem of the damp shirt around and around her index finger. "Has there been anyone else?"

"Does it matter?"

Kate shrugged and studied her fingers. "Yes—no." She rolled her eyes, despising herself because it did matter. "I'm just curious."

He tipped up her chin until her gaze met his. "There have been other women, but you spoiled me for anyone else."

Kate stared, her heart lodged in her throat. Did he mean he loved her still? No, she told herself sternly. He hadn't said he loved her, and if he *did* love her, he would have to tell her so. But they'd made progress and for the time being, at least, she would satisfy herself with that.

She glanced at her watch. "Maybe you'd better take me back to my car now."

His hands closed over hers, stilling their nervous movement. She lifted her gaze to his face. Need stretched taut between them. With a quick tug on her wrists, he had her body pressed flush against his. His hands moved to the underside of her knees and began to slide slowly upward. "Why?"

The sensual climb of his fingertips quickened Kate's breathing. "Because…it's late and I…still have to find a motel."

His fingers inched the fabric of the shirt up the back of her legs. "Why don't you stay here?"

Heat radiated between their bodies, warming Kate's front side, while goose bumps popped up on the back of her legs exposed to the cool air. Oh, how she wanted to curl up in his lap and say yes, but what would tomorrow bring? Would there be regrets? All her emotions were so close to the surface, she didn't feel she could trust them. And what about him? There was no questioning the fact that he wanted her—she could feel his hardness against her thigh. But what was he really offering her? She had a right to know. "And where would I sleep?"

Chase shrugged. "There's only one bed."

She caught him by the elbows and pulled his arms from their sensual trailing. "Are you asking me to sleep with you?"

With his arms held in her grasp, Chase knew he was

trapped. He could break free from her hold, but suspected he couldn't escape her probing as easily.

"Yeah, I guess so." Without conscious thought, he held his breath, hoping she'd drop the inquisition.

"Are you offering me a night in your bed, or more?"

He let out his breath in a soft, defeated whoosh. "What do you mean by 'more'?"

Kate felt a warm blush work its way up her neck. He knew what she wanted to know. Why was he making this so difficult? "I mean… Do you love me?"

The muscles in Chase's jaw tightened. He wanted her, of that he was sure. But did he love her? Seven years ago he could have answered that question without batting an eye, but now he couldn't say the words she wanted to hear.

They both needed time. A chance to get to know each other again. The words meant too much for him to say just to get her in his bed. Feelings came slow for him. And trust even slower.

"I don't know." He felt her tense at his words. He gripped her shoulders and forced her to listen. "I know I want you and I know I care about you, but that's all I can offer you right now."

She pushed away from him and moved to stand with her face to the fire, her back stiff and unbending. "I think you'd better take me back now."

He glared at her back, then rose and walked to the window. He stared, frowning, out at the rain. "I hate to tell you this, Kate," he said after a moment. "But you aren't going anywhere tonight."

Her eyes widened and her jaw went slack as she turned to look at Chase.

"We're stranded." He jerked his thumb in the direction of the window. "See for yourself."

She moved to his side and peered out the window to the darkness beyond. A flash of lightning exposed the yard outside. The cabin seemed to be floating in the middle of a lake. Even the rock drive leading from the road to the cabin had disappeared beneath the flood of rainwater. "Oh, no! How're we going to get out of here?"

"We're not." Chase moved to take her place before the fireplace, his hands clasped behind him. Then he laughed.

Kate wheeled to face him. "This isn't funny."

"I'm sorry. But you should see your face. You'd think I'd planned this whole setup." The heat began to warm his back, and he stepped away from the fire. "As soon as the rain stops, the water'll run off pretty fast, but it'll be morning before we'll be able to drive out."

He left her standing at the window and disappeared into the bedroom. He returned with a blanket and a pillow. "I'll take the sofa, and you can have the bed." After tossing the bedding onto the sofa, he crossed his arms in front of him and, with a jerk upward, peeled off his sweatshirt.

Kate watched him in angry silence. When his fingers reached for the snap of his jeans, she sucked in a breath and bolted for the bedroom door.

With her finger laden with toothpaste, Kate frowned into the silvered mirror above the bathroom sink. The eyes that looked back at her were fever bright, the face flushed and the lips swollen. She placed her hand on the soft fabric covering her breast and felt the sharp point of her nipple, hard and erect beneath her fingers. Her fingers rubbed lightly back and forth across the engorged peak as she remembered the feel of Chase's body pressed against hers.

Stop this!

She jammed her toothpaste-laden finger into her mouth and rubbed her teeth until her finger ached from the effort. She couldn't allow herself to think this way. She wasn't about to become physically involved with him again. Not without some kind of commitment on his part.

She frowned into the mirror. He'd planned this, she just knew he had. How could he *not* know the creek would rise, flooding the land and trapping them here? She spit into the sink, filled her mouth with water and spit again. Darn him!

Still fuming, she stomped into the bedroom and flipped back the quilt. Sliding under the mountain of homemade quilts piled on the bed, she sunk into a feather mattress... and smiled.

There was some satisfaction in knowing that Chase was stretched on the lumpy, uncomfortable sofa, while she was ensconced in feathers. Serves him right, she thought smugly as she turned onto her side and plumped the pillow with her fist. With a deep sigh, she closed her eyes and relaxed.

But sleep evaded her. Lingering scents of Chase surrounded her. On the pillow, on the sheets, even on the shirt she wore. She imagined him as he'd looked when he'd pulled his sweatshirt over his head, baring his chest to her before reaching for the snap on his jeans.

She flopped over onto her back, glared at the ceiling, and began counting sheep. One. Two. Three. Four... As she counted, her eyes grew heavy with the monotony, and the vision of animals leaping over the fence slowly changed from sheep to cows. Twenty-two. Twenty-three. Twenty-four. A bull appeared on the opposite side of the fence. Kate's eyes grew heavier and heavier. Thirty-six. Thirty-seven. All the cows floated away until only one cow remained. The cow leapt over the fence and slowly the bull ambled toward her, muscles rippling, power radiating in each slow, earth-jarring step....

Seven

A crash outside the bedroom window startled Kate to full wakefulness. Hugging the covers to her breasts, she sat up in bed and glanced around the pitch-black room, momentarily disoriented. Then she remembered—she was with Chase at his cabin in the woods. More than a little frightened, she dragged a quilt from the bed and scuttled to the front room where Chase slept. The loud noise had not awakened him and Kate refused to, dreading his derision more than the storm.

With the quilt wrapped tightly around her, she lay down on the rag rug in front of the fireplace, feeling safe in Chase's nearness.

Only a few red coals remained in the fireplace, offering little warmth to the chilly room. Chase pulled the quilt up over his shoulder and huddled closer to the back of the sofa, but it wasn't enough. He kicked off the covers, swung his bare feet to the cold floor and stumbled to the fireplace to throw on another log.

His foot caught on something and he lunged forward, his arms swinging to gain balance.

"Ow-w-w!" Kate screamed.

"What in the hell are you doing in the middle of the floor?" Chase bellowed furiously, glaring down at Kate's crumpled form on the floor.

With her fingers pressed against her rib cage, Kate shouted back, "What in the hell are *you* doing prancing around in the dark?"

"I wasn't prancing around. I was going to add wood to the fire. And why aren't you in bed?"

Embarrassed at her cowardice, Kate lifted her chin defensively. "Lightning struck something outside and it crashed against my window. When I came to see if you heard it, too, you were asleep." She lifted a shoulder in an indifferent shrug. "Rather than wake you, I decided to just sleep here." She pulled the quilt up over her shoulder and stated indignantly, "And I was sleeping just fine until you nearly trampled me to death."

Chase stood in his briefs, his hands pushing at his hips. When Kate finished her explanation, he threw back his head and laughed at the ceiling.

"What's so funny?" Kate demanded.

"You are," Chase sputtered, still laughing. "I can't imagine a grown woman leaving a warm bed to sleep on the cold, hard floor because she was scared."

He turned, picked up some dry kindling and threw it on the coals. They caught and flamed, illuminating Chase in their reddish glow, turning his bronze skin a burnished copper. His hair was as black as a moonless night and mussed from sleep. When he stooped to throw a log on the fire, muscles tightened on his behind, leaving dimpled indentations on his briefs.

Kate attempted to swallow the lump building in her throat, threatening to cut off her air. She had to get out of this room! She struggled to her feet, fighting with the quilt to free her tangled limbs. Her struggles stopped and she grasped her side, groaning.

Chase wheeled and immediately stepped to her side. "What's wrong?" he asked, placing his hand over hers.

"You stepped on my ribs, and it hurts." In the firelight, Kate's face paled and her lips pinched.

He slowly unwound the quilt from her body. As his finger eased the shirt up to inspect her injuries, he brushed a knuckle against her bare skin and she sucked in a breath. With gentle fingers, he skillfully ran his hands along her ribs, inadvertently sweeping against the swell of her breast in his search for broken bones. When the cold air had hit her bare skin, it had chilled her, but nothing could cool the heat building inside, sparked by his touch.

"I don't think anything's broken. Does it still hurt?" His fingers gently massaged the skin beneath her breast.

She opened her mouth to answer, but nothing came out. She cleared her throat and tried again, this time her voice came low and husky. "Only when I move."

Chase tucked the quilt around her shoulders. "Wrap your arms around my neck, and I'll carry you back to bed." He ducked his head to peer into her eyes. "Tell me if I hurt you, all right?"

Still tingling from his touch, her breath came out in a breathless whisper. "All right."

He slipped one arm beneath her knees and the other around her back, until his hand rested against the fullness of her breast. With great care, he lifted her and carried her back to the bedroom.

She sank into the soft feathers of the mattress as he slowly pulled away his hands. He tucked the piles of quilts around her and leaned over. "Do you need anything before I go back to bed? Aspirin, hot water bottle...?" His voice drifted off when he ran out of things to offer her.

Yes, you, her heart cried, but she replied softly, "No."

Chase turned and walked toward the door.

Kate glanced nervously around the shadowed room and listened as the wind howled through the trees surrounding the small cabin. She attempted to swallow the lump of fear lodged in her throat. "Chase?"

He paused at the door and glanced back over his shoulder. "Yeah?"

She swallowed again...this time her pride. Her voice came small and shaky from the depths of the quilts. "Would you sleep with me?"

Lightning flashed, and their eyes met. Chase studied her in that split second of illumination. What was she asking of him? Just a reassuring presence in her bed? After what she'd said earlier, he could only assume that was all.

He retraced his steps, his bare feet padding softly on the cold hardwood floor. With an impatient gruffness in his voice, he said, "Scoot over." He slipped under the quilts, then flopped over, turning his back to Kate.

She frowned at the broad expanse and inched closer, until she felt the heat radiating from his body. Content, she closed her eyes and waited for sleep to come.

* * *

Morning brought sunlight streaming through the undraped window, its rays slanting across Chase's face. He slowly awakened and grimaced in pain. He twisted his head to look at his arm, which was pinned beneath Kate's head. It felt like lead.

With a gentle tug, he eased it from beneath her, then crooked it, propped his cheek on the heel of his hand and watched her sleep. Auburn tresses cascaded across her face, spilling over onto his chest. He lifted her hair up and back from her face. Long, thick lashes lay like fringe beneath her closed eyes. She looked so innocent, so like the young woman he'd married. Unable to resist, he touched his lips to her eyelids, then brushed his lips across her lightly freckled nose. He leaned back with a smile. So it was makeup. The freckles he'd remembered still dotted her nose.

He scooted down the mattress until his face leveled with hers, and he nipped at her lips with his teeth.

She batted a slow hand at the irritating intrusion to her sleep, but swatted only air when he reared back. When she'd settled her hand back between her cheek and pillow, Chase circled her with an arm, drew near once again and pressed his lips against hers.

With a contented sigh, Kate lifted an arm and draped it loosely around his neck. She murmured sleepily, "Don't wake me. I'm having the best dream."

A low chuckle came from deep in Chase's throat. "What about?"

"I can't tell until after breakfast or it won't come true."

"Must be good."

She snuggled closer, pressing her body to match the curves

in his. "Mmm-hmm." She lifted her hands to his chest and drew tiny circles with her fingernails.

It was almost his undoing. With a deep groan, he rolled to his back, pulling Kate on top of him. His eyes burned with a challenge as they met hers. "If you don't intend to finish what you're starting, then you'd better climb out of this bed right now." Without moving his eyes from hers, he moved his left hand to press her hips against his. "I need you, Kate."

I need you, Kate? She suppressed a laugh. It wasn't necessary to voice his *need*...she felt the strength of it pressing against the *V* of her legs. And she saw it in his eyes, bright with the fever of passion.

And she needed him. For seven years she'd buried that need and had fought that need since the first time she'd seen him again at the hotel. But now she was lying in his arms, in his bed, and it felt so right, more right than anything had in years. She wanted Chase Morgan as much as he wanted her.

Fully aware of the implications of her movements, she sat up, her buttocks pressed against his thighs, her knees squeezing him from either side, and crossed her arms in front of her. Grabbing her shirt by the hem, she slowly pulled it over her head.

It was all the answer Chase needed. With an impatient groan, he reached up and covered her breasts with his hands, cupping and kneading, warming them until her nipples stood erect. Like a child in a room full of new toys, he didn't know what to touch or play with first. He wanted all of her.

He slid his hands down the smooth skin of her stomach until they reached the elastic of her silk bikini panties. Easing the elastic back, he trailed his fingers in a slow path around her, his soft touch causing Kate to arch her back in sweet anticipation. When his fingers met at the small of her back, he slid his hands beneath the silk fabric and dug his fingers into the soft flesh of her buttocks, removing the panties and drawing a deep groan from low in Kate's throat.

Her head fell back and her fingers gripped his shoulders as waves of pleasure washed over her. With a seductive smile, she returned her gaze to Chase and pulled her fingers down his chest, raking his nipples with her nails in her downward path.

Chase moaned in pleasure as his eyes drifted closed. He pulled Kate down beside him, then held her at arm's length while he devoured her with his eyes. "God, you're beautiful." With an almost reverent touch, he placed his fingers at her lips, then dragged them in a slow path downward. "I've thought about you, *dreamed* about you, for seven years, but my dreams don't hold a candle to the real thing."

Kate's heart swelled until she thought it would burst. To her ears, Shakespeare couldn't have said it more eloquently. Chase had never stopped thinking about her, just as she had never stopped thinking about him. And he was talking, sharing his innermost thoughts with her.

"I want you, Kate," he whispered, kicking free of his briefs. He flung a knee across her upper legs and rose until he knelt above her. Lowering his body over hers, he covered her face and neck in a flurry of quick, burning kisses. He wanted to possess her, make her his, erase the memory of another man's touch. He snaked his lips in a downward path until he reached her nipples.

And Kate wanted him. All of him. She arched her back, thrusting her breasts upward to meet him, greedy for the feel of his lips, for his touch. He circled an engorged peak, then slowly drew it into his mouth and suckled, first one breast, then the other, until Kate thought she'd go mad from her need for him.

"Chase." Her breath came in quick gasps while her fingers dug into his shoulders. "Please. Now."

Slowly, he eased into her, as if this were her first time and he feared he might hurt her. The tenderness of the gesture had tears burning the back of her throat and her fingers threading through his hair, but then her breath caught as the hard fullness of his arousal stretched her until she covered him like a velvet glove. The room spun around her in a dizzying kaleidoscope of color as she arched to meet him, urging him deeper and deeper, hugging him to her until they were like one.

He began a rhythmic urging, gradually picking up the pace and drawing her closer and closer to a deep chasm, then slowly pulling her away. Their lips met and tangled, each whispering words of passion and pleasure to the other.

Her hands seemed to float over his heated skin with a mind of their own. Across the breadth of his shoulders, down the muscled plains of his back to his hips, feeling the constriction of the muscles on his buttocks as he moved above her.

For the first time in years, Kate felt like she was making love—not just fulfilling a duty. When she thought she could stand no more, that she would surely die of her need for him, Chase plunged deep within her, crushing her hips against him, pushing her over the edge into a spiraling dive of pleasure.

Perspiration beaded his skin. Kate tasted the salt with her lips pressed against his shoulder. Their passion spent, they continued to hold each other, not wanting to end the sense of oneness their lovemaking had brought them.

Slowly, Chase raised himself from Kate and supported his weight with the palms of his hands pressed on either side of her. "I've waited seven years for this," he said, his breathing still labored, "and it may take me another seven years to get the energy to repeat it." He groaned and pushed himself over to fall exhausted at her side, one arm flung across her waist, the other dangling over the edge of the bed.

Kate turned beneath the weight of his arm to face him and began to run her fingernails up and down his chest. "Seven years?" she asked in a seductive whisper. "I thought you were made of stronger stuff than that, Chase Morgan."

Slowly he turned his head to look at her. A wicked grin chipped at one corner of his mouth. Without warning, he grabbed her, pinning her hands between their chests. He rolled across the bed, coming to a stop with Kate beneath him.

"We'll see who's made of stronger stuff," he threatened in a low voice. He then began a slow and thorough exploration of Kate's body, leaving her breathless and writhing beneath him.

A fire blazed in the fireplace, casting a glow on the two lovers entwined on the couch. Like two sated cats, they stretched and purred in contentment and snuggled closer to one another. They had left the feather bed with the best of intentions, but had made it only as far as the sofa. They had seven years' worth of loving to make up for, and seemed determined to make it up in one day.

"We aren't fit to kill, you know it?" Chase said in a lazy voice.

"Mmm-hmm."

"Let's go fishing."

Kate lifted her head a fraction from his chest and looked at him through narrowed eyes. "You've got to be kidding."

A broad grin spread across Chase's face as he warmed to the idea. He whacked her on the bottom and slid from beneath her. "Whoever catches the biggest fish doesn't have to clean them or cook. Deal?"

Kate dropped her cheek onto the cushion still warm from

Chase's body and prayed she'd win. She didn't know a gill from a tail fin and wasn't anxious to learn.

Kate trudged behind Chase, her feet making sucking sounds in the mud as she walked. She glanced at his back, his broad shoulders, then at the fishing hat cocked far back on his head. Lures dangled from the canvas hat's faded band. Her lips dipped into a frown as she waited expectantly for him at any moment to burst into song. How could anyone enjoy being out in this cold, damp air? she wondered as a shiver shook her shoulders.

She pulled the too big army jacket closer around her with her free hand and hugged the tackle box with the other. Why had she allowed him to talk her into this? She didn't know beans about fishing and she'd much rather be snuggled up in front of the fireplace than traipsing through the muck.

Pines towered above them, and a light wind occasionally showered raindrops from their laden boughs. Kate and Chase had walked quite a distance through the woods before the trees began to thin and the path turned abruptly to the left. A small lake appeared before them as if miraculously produced from the hand of an illusionist. The afternoon sun glistened on the water, turning its smooth surface to glass. Kate breathed deeply of the fresh, pine-scented air.

"This is beautiful," she whispered in deference to the stillness surrounding them.

"My favorite fishing hole." Chase knelt at the weathered pier and reached for the tackle box. He snapped it open and began to dig through the tangle of lines, hooks and lures.

The weather-grayed boards listed under Kate's feet as she strolled across the pier. The peacefulness and the beauty of the secluded lake chased away her earlier mood, and she was glad Chase had forced her to come. She sat down at the end of the pier cross-legged and glanced back over her shoulder. "Hurry up, slowpoke," she demanded with a cocky smile. "I've got some serious fishing to do."

With the fishing rods gripped in one hand and the tackle box in the other, Chase stepped onto the laddered walkway, the barrels suspending it pitching and rolling under his added weight. "Do you know how to cast?" he asked as he made his way toward her.

"Only a play," she replied, laughing. "Maybe you better throw it out, then I'll hold it."

After casting out her line and then his, Chase settled down beside her, their shoulders brushing.

"What do I do now?"

"Just sit back and wait. If you feel a tug on your line, let me know."

And wait she did. Patiently, at first, but as time passed, she became fidgety. "How long does it take?"

Chase smiled and shook his head as he fingered his line. "Don't know. Fish are funny. Sometimes they bite, sometimes they don't. There've been times I hooked one as soon as my line hit the water. Others when I'd fish all day and never catch a thing."

Kate pushed her shoulders down in dejection. Chase chuckled at her lack of patience and scooted closer so he could drape an arm around her.

She relaxed against him. "Do you come here often?"

"When I want to get away."

"Away from what?"

His shoulders rubbed against hers in a shrug. "Problems. I come here to gain perspective."

"Have you been here all week?"

Chase tucked his chin against his chest to look down at her. "How'd you know I've been gone all week?"

Kate glanced out across the lake, enjoying the peacefulness and understanding his desire to escape to here. "I've been trying to find you, and Mrs. Kimbrough told me you were out of town. What made you lose perspective this time?"

Chase slid his arm down to her waist and fitted her snugly up against him. Kate glanced over and found him smiling down at her. "A redhead."

"Me?" she asked incredulously.

"Yeah, you. You really get under my skin, lady."

"What did I do?"

"Nothing…and everything."

Kate frowned up at him. "What's that supposed to mean?"

He pulled his arm from around her and hugged his knees. "You came back."

"So?"

He squinted his eyes up at the sun, then turned his gaze on Kate. "It took me a long time to accept losing you, then, there you were again."

Before Kate could reply, her line jerked hard, nearly ripping the rod from her grip. She jumped to her feet. "Chase! I think I caught one."

He eased away from her, studying her line as he went. "Not till it's in the frying pan. First, you have to set the hook. Give him a little line to play with. Easy now. Looks like a big one. Okay, now lock your reel."

She turned to him with a puzzled look. "What?"

"Just turn the crank handle until it clicks. That's good. Now give your rod a jerk and set the hook."

Kate did and received a smile from Chase. "Good girl. Now start reeling him in."

She slowly turned the handle while Chase knelt at the foot of the pier with a net. Her rod began to bend under the strain. "Oh, Chase, it's going to break!"

"No, it won't. It's fiberglass. Just keep reeling him in."

The fish broke through the water, flipping and fighting against the hook. Chase squatted down and leaned over the edge of the pier to scoop it into the net. "Well, I'll be darned. Looks like you caught the granddaddy," he declared in a proud voice. "Five pounds if he's an ounce." He spun on the balls of his feet and held the bass up for Kate's inspection.

She dropped the rod and reel and jumped up and down, squealing. "I did it. Chase, I did it." Then she threw herself at him, wrapping her arms around his neck and her legs around his waist. The lunge caught Chase off balance and he thrust a hand out to stop his backward fall, but grabbed only air.

Chase, Kate and the net holding the granddaddy bass all hit the water at the same time.

The weekend passed quickly, the isolation and seclusion of the cabin offering them a chance to get to know one another again without interruptions or reminders of the past or pressures of the present.

Sunday afternoon, they returned to First Monday in Canton and the parking lot where Kate had left her car.

Chase stood at the car door as she prepared to leave for Dallas, listening while she gave him the directions to the Mor-Lang development, where he was to drop off the furniture.

"Are you sure you don't want me to follow and help you unload?"

"No. I can manage." He leaned through the car window and kissed her. As he started to pull his head back, Kate reached out, laced her fingers behind his neck and pulled him back in for another.

"You better get out of here before I drag you back to the cabin," Chase warned in a husky voice.

She batted her eyes at him seductively. "Sounds good to me."

He whacked the car roof with his palm, then smiled. "Scoot! I'll come over when I finish."

She stuck her hand out the window and waved as she headed for I-20 and Dallas.

Kate grabbed the phone on the first ring. Her fingers shook from the combined effects of too much coffee, too little sleep, and a whole lot of nerves.

"Kate, this is Joe Langford."

She sagged against the wall of her kitchen. She'd hoped to hear Chase's voice. "Hi, Joe. What can I do for you?"

"My partner wants you to meet him at two o'clock at the models. Bring your sketches and samples. He wants a full report."

"Is something wrong?" Kate asked, noting the agitated tone in his voice.

"I don't know yet. He called me this morning in a rage. All hell's broken loose at the property and heads are rolling. I don't know why he wants you. I'm just following orders."

"Thanks, Joe. I'll be there."

Kate grabbed receipts, sketches, fabric selections, wallpaper samples, paint samples and floor plans, and worried the whole time she was doing it.

Have I done something wrong? She ticked through her

memory, looking for a mistake she might have made. Joe had approved everything she'd done thus far. She'd stayed within the budget she'd been given. Why in the world did Joe's partner want to see her? She'd worked for Mor-Lang for over a week and had never laid eyes on the man. So why now?

The fact that she hadn't slept well the night before heightened her nervousness. She'd waited until past midnight for Chase to come by, finally giving up and going to bed. Visions of automobile accidents, engine trouble and a hundred other calamities kept her tossing and turning all night. Under the shadow of darkness, she finally concluded he didn't care. He'd gotten what he wanted—Kate McGinis in his bed.

After sleeping fitfully for a few hours, she'd received Joe's call.

I don't need this today, she fretted as she sped toward the propertion and her appointment with the mysterious partner.

She pulled up in front of the contractor's office. Expecting to see George, the security guard, she was surprised when a big, burly man approached her car.

"Hi, I'm Kate McGinis."

The man glanced down at the clipboard he held in his hand, then turned and pointed over the hood of the car. "The boss is over in Section II at Model No. 3." Looking down his nose at her, he added, "Beware. He's on a tear today."

Kate gave him a weak smile. "Thanks for the warning." She rolled up her window and pulled the gearshift down. "All right," she murmured beneath her breath. "Here I come, ready or not."

When she entered Model No. 3, she heard loud voices and followed the sound to the French doors leading to the backyard. Two men, one dressed in work clothes and the other in a Western suit, stood in the middle of the yard. The man in the suit had his back to Kate, but his stance was all too familiar. Every sentence he spoke was punctuated with a finger jabbed at the chest of the workman. The sick feeling that had whirled in her stomach since awakening quickly rose to tighten her throat.

"No, it can't be," she told herself. Her hand shaking, she opened the door and stepped out into the brisk air.

"Chase?" she called as she made her way toward him. "What are you doing here?"

"Waiting for you."

"But I was supposed to meet my employer…" At the guilty look in his eyes, all hope melted from her, leaving her feeling limp and defeated, but more than anything, cheated. "You're my employer?"

"Yes." He squared his shoulders and waited for the explosion he knew was bound to follow.

"But…but," she sputtered helplessly. "I thought you worked for my landlord."

"I do…in a way. I own Vision Properties—the same company that owns your house. I'm also co-owner of Mor-Lang, Inc."

Her fingers pressed tight against her temples, Kate squeezed her eyes shut, hoping that this was all a bad dream. When she opened them, Chase still stood before her, his mouth twisted to one side, and looking as guilty as hell. She turned away.

All this time he'd allowed her to think he worked as a repairman for her landlord. All those conversations they'd had over the weeks about trust. She felt so foolish. So deceived. The nausea quickly churned itself into anger, and she wheeled to face him. "Why did you lie to me?"

"I never lied."

"What would you call it then?" she demanded. "I've been living in your house for almost two months and didn't know you owned it, and I've been working for you and didn't know you were my employer. If that isn't deceit, I'd like to know what it is!"

Chase knew this was coming and was prepared to deal with it. "Come on, Kate, let's go inside and talk." He reached for her arm, but she jerked away from him.

"Don't touch me," she threatened.

With his jaw set in a determined line, he grabbed her by the elbow and pushed her into the house in front of him. "I've had about all I'm going to take from everyone today, including you. And you *will* listen if I have to hog-tie you to do it."

Eight

Once inside, Kate snatched her elbow from his grasp and folded her arms tight across her chest as she moved away from him. Tears burned the back of her eyes, but she refused to cry. She felt so foolish. All this time she'd thought he was nothing but a blue-collar worker. How he must be enjoying this marvelous joke. Not only her employer, but her landlord, as well!

"I never lied to you, Kate. You never asked me what I did for a living. You just assumed I was the repairman for Vision Properties. As for you working for me, well…" he conceded, "I did sort of arrange that. I had Mrs. Kimbrough tell you about the opening for the job. But your leasing one of my houses was just fate. I had nothing to do with that. When Mrs. Kimbrough brought me the lease agreement, I was as surprised as you are right now."

He paused to let this sink in, then stuffed his hands deep

into the pockets of his slacks, jingling change. "I live about three blocks from you, so when you had electrical problems, Mrs. Kimbrough just naturally called me to check it out. If you'll remember, you never asked why I was there. You just took it for granted that I was the repairman."

Kate's chin quivered as she fought the need to cry. "Why did you arrange this job?"

He tipped his head to study the toe of his boots. "After seeing you again, I was curious. I didn't know why you'd decided to reappear in my life, but I didn't want to lose you again until I had a chance to find out. So—" he shrugged his shoulders, still without looking at her "—I decided to give you the job to make sure you stayed in Dallas for a while. But I didn't create the job for you," he added defensively, glancing up at her. "It was Joe's idea. He's been hounding me for a long time to hire someone. It seemed the perfect solution to both problems."

Though his explanation seemed believable, the pain of being manipulated again wouldn't allow Kate to forgive him. "Why didn't you tell me before now? We just spent an entire weekend together. Surely you could've found the time."

He pulled his hands from his pockets and stepped closer to pull Kate's hands into his. "I didn't want to ruin the weekend. I knew if I told you, you'd blow up, and that would destroy a perfect opportunity for us to get to know each other again. Don't cry, Kate."

Jerking her hands from his, she turned away and rubbed the back of her hands beneath her eyes. "I'm not crying." Memories of the weekend whirled through her mind. Cooking together, laughing together…making love together. In a shaky voice, she said, "I need time to think this through."

He took a step toward her, then stopped himself. "Don't you think you're overreacting a little bit?"

She wheeled to face him, her eyes bright with unshed tears. "Overreacting? No, I think I'm handling this really well considering I didn't have any sleep last night. I walked the floor all night, worrying about you! I imagined automobile accidents and you lying in some hospital hurt." This time she couldn't stop the tears. They spilled over her lids and down her cheeks.

"I'm sorry, Kate. It never occurred to me that you'd wait up."

"Just like it never occurred to you seven years ago that I'd worry about you when you didn't come home."

"Let's not go into that again."

"Okay, forget the past. What about last night? Why didn't you come to my house like you said you would?"

Chase leaned one shoulder against the wall and crossed one boot over the other. "When I drove in last night to drop off the furniture, I discovered someone had vandalized Section II. Windows were broken, paint spattered on the walls, carpet and appliances were stolen."

That news temporarily robbed Kate of her anger with Chase. "Where was George?"

"On duty, just like he was supposed to be." Chase slammed a balled fist against the wall. "They hit him over the head with a brick and tied him up while they destroyed the place. He's going to be all right," he answered to the concern he saw on her face. "He's over at Parkland Hospital. They're keeping him a few days for observation and testing, but it seems he suffered only a mild concussion. They took a few stitches to close the wound. I stayed with him until he went to sleep and didn't get home until about four this morning."

The security guard was okay, Chase had seen to that. But what about her? Kate rubbed her fingers wearily across her forehead as she turned away. "Do you see history repeating itself here?"

Chase frowned, watching her back. "No."

She turned to look at him, her eyes dulled by a sadness she couldn't explain. "Don't you think you could have picked up the phone and called me and let me know what was going on?"

A muscle twitched on his jaw. "I'm not used to checking in with anyone."

"It's not 'checking in,' it's called common courtesy. Try it sometime." Kate threw up her hands. "Oh, never mind." She paced away, then returned, pushing back the anger and squaring her shoulders. "I assume your summons for me to meet you here has something to do with the vandalism."

His frown deepening, Chase said, "Yeah."

"Isn't this a little more than the usual pilfering that goes on at a construction site?"

His lips thinned. "Seems to be. That's why I wanted to talk to you. I don't want you out here working alone. If you need to come to the site, call Joe and he'll make arrangements for someone to meet you and stay with you until you're through. *Never* come out after dark or alone!

"And I want you to make your interior selections on all the houses as fast as possible. I've doubled the crews in order to get the mess cleaned up and put us back on schedule. You need to make arrangements with the paperhangers, the painters, the carpet layers and anybody else you need to walk in the minute the carpenters are finished. We have exactly three weeks before our grand opening, and I plan to be ready."

He walked toward Kate, narrowing the distance between

them. "I have to catch a flight to Austin this afternoon, so I'm depending on you and Joe to keep things running on schedule."

Kate stared at him in dismay. "Austin? Aren't you needed here?"

"Yes, but I've been working on a renovation for a city block in downtown Dallas. The city council already approved it, but because it includes an historical area, I've had to work through both federal and state agencies. Everything was going great until this morning." He combed his fingers through his hair, then frowned and jammed his hands deep into his pockets. "All of a sudden some legislators in Austin are breathing down my neck and throwing red tape all over me. I've got to go down and get it straightened out. Time is money, and they're costing me a bundle with these holdups."

He stepped in front of Kate and took her elbows in his hands. "I hate to leave right now. We need to talk...about us."

He felt her stiffen.

"I'm not sure we have anything else to say to each other."

"Kate, I know you're upset."

She shook free and took a step back, putting distance between them. "No. Please. In the future, I think it would be best if we kept our relationship strictly business." She turned and walked away.

Torn, but knowing that time might be to his advantage, Chase let her go.

The following week was one of frustration and disappointment for Kate. The confrontation with Chase proved to be only the tip of the iceberg. Two of the proposals she presented to businesses were turned down. Then her lawyer called to inform her there would be a delay in receiving her settlement from her divorce from Philip.

Needing something positive to boost her morale, she picked up the phone and dialed the number of a law firm she was working with to determine the status on her only outstanding bid.

"Fellows, Goodhart and Simpson," the receptionist said.

"Mr. Fellows, please."

"And whom may I say is calling?"

"Kate McGinis." She crossed her fingers and waited for what seemed like an eternity.

Mr. Fellows's voice cracked across the line. "Ms. McGinis, how can I help you?"

"Hello, Mr. Fellows. I'm calling to check on my bid. Has your firm reached a decision on my proposal yet?"

There was a slight pause, then Mr. Fellows cleared his throat. "Uh, yes, we have." He cleared his throat again, obviously uncomfortable. "The partners of the firm met and approved the proposal of another company."

Kate's lips trembled, but she forced her voice to remain steady and businesslike. "Why did they refuse my proposal? Were my suggestions too drastic or my bid too high?"

"No. No, your suggestions were both practical and economical."

"Then I don't understand. What was the problem?"

She heard Mr. Fellows's sigh. He lowered his voice to reply. "Confidentially, Ms. McGinis, the decision was made after a great deal of controversy and debate. I'm sorry your bid was rejected. Personally, I feel your suggestions were more appropriate and more in line with our budget."

"Thank you, Mr. Fellows. Well, maybe next time."

As Kate replaced the receiver, tears flowed down her face. The combined disappointments of the other rejections surfaced and boiled over. "What's happening here?" she cried. "I'm working my buns off and getting nothing but rejections."

There was no one to answer her and no one to console her. She needed Chase. That thought brought a fresh wave of tears. "Not only my business, but my personal life is a failure, too." She fell back onto the couch, sobbing out the misery and frustrations.

The phone rang. Grabbing a tissue from the coffee table, she blew her nose and wiped at the tears on her cheeks.

"Hello?" she sniffed.

"Kate? You sound terrible! Are you sick?"

"No, I'm not sick," she said as fresh tears flooded her eyes at the sound of concern in her sister's voice.

"I'm on my way."

"Don't come, Becca." There was a click and then silence. "Becca?" Kate tapped the toggle switch. "Becca?" She slammed the receiver down. "Darn you, Becca. I don't need you," she grumbled. But deep down she was really relieved. It always helped to talk out problems with someone. She glanced around the empty room. And there was certainly no one here.

She wandered listlessly around the house while she waited for Becca, starting several projects, then dropping them in disinterest.

An hour passed before Becca burst into the house carrying a huge grocery bag. "The recovery team has arrived!" she called merrily to Kate.

Kate looked from Becca to the bag she clutched in her hands and pointed at the bag. "What's in there? Razor blades? A straitjacket? Or maybe some cyanide capsules?"

"Oo-oo. A little black humor, huh, Kate?" Without waiting for a reply, Becca marched to the center of the living room and, wearing an impish grin, clutched the bag to her chest. "What did we do when we were teenagers and were depressed?"

"I'm not in the mood to travel down memory lane," Kate said with a warning frown.

Becca ignored her. "We put on our sloppiest clothes, hugged our favorite stuffed animal and *ate!*"

She dug in the bag, pulling out a faded sweatshirt and threw it at Kate. Giggling, she lifted out a ragged teddy bear, minus one eye and with one ear hanging by a thread. "Your teddy bear. And last, but not least," she said, turning the sack upside down and dumping the contents on the living room floor. "Chocolate. A surefire cure for everything!"

Kate stared wide-eyed at the wild assortment littering her floor. Oreo cookies, Hershey's, Snickers, chocolate covered peanuts and Fudgsicles?

Becca scooped up the box of Fudgsicles and headed for the kitchen. "I'll put these in the freezer. They're for dessert."

Snatching up the bag of Oreos, Kate flopped down on the couch. "I can almost feel the zits these delicacies are going to produce."

"Get in the spirit of things," Becca ordered as she returned. "Put on your sweatshirt."

Grudgingly, Kate pulled the worn shirt over her silk blouse. She looked up just in time to catch the teddy bear Becca threw to her.

Kate held the bear aloft and stared at him in disbelief. "Where in the world did you find Honey Bear?"

"Mother sent over all my old memory boxes when Dan and I moved into our house. Honey Bear was in one of them."

After ripping the wrapper off a candy bar, Becca plopped down in a chair and pulled her feet under her. "Now tell me why you're so upset."

Kate hugged Honey Bear to her and nibbled halfheartedly at a cookie. "I don't know where to begin. The entire week's been a nightmare."

"Start at the beginning."

By her third cookie, Kate warmed to her story and held Becca spellbound with a recap of the visit with Mor-Lang's silent partner, alias Chase Walden Morgan, and the disappointments of her business.

"Wow! You have had a bad week."

"Yes, and the problem is, I don't know how to resolve any of it. I'm working my butt off, but the only money I'm making is from Mor-Lang." Kate propped her chin on the teddy bear's head. "The heck of it is, if it weren't for Chase, I could probably apply for welfare."

Her forehead wrinkled thoughtfully, Becca wadded up her candy wrapper and began to lick the chocolate from her fingers. "I hate to say it, but this all sounds vaguely familiar."

"What do you mean?"

"After your divorce, didn't all your bids in Washington get rejected?"

"Yes, but I know who caused that."

"Exactly."

"You mean, you think Philip is behind this?"

"Why not? He's certainly devious enough. Think back a minute. Didn't you have an argument when he came here to see you?"

"Well…yes…sort of." She tried to recall her conversation with Philip. "He said something about me regretting

the day I'd compared him to a ditch digger—he was referring to Chase."

Becca gave Kate a smug smile. "There's your answer."

For a moment there was silence, then Kate shook her head.
"No, he had the connections in Washington to pull that off,
but not here."

"You've got to be kidding! Political lines intersect every
major city in the United States. You've lived in that circle,
Kate. Surely you must see the possibilities."

Kate picked at the fuzz balls on the ragged bear as she considered the likelihood. "You may be right." Kate's anger built as
she pictured Philip's invisible hand maneuvering her life again.
"It also explains this sudden delay in our property settlement.
That scheming, conniving, son of a— I could wring his neck."

"Atta girl, Kate," Becca squealed as she clapped her hands.
"But don't get mad, get even."

The anger whooshed out of Kate like the air out of a
balloon, leaving her limp and lifeless. "How?"

Becca flipped her hands, palms up. "I don't know. You know
your business better than I do. Aren't there ways you can make
money and bide your time until Philip tires of this vendetta?"

"Maybe." Kate rose and began to pace back and forth in
front of Becca's chair. "I've been going after corporate
accounts. I need to focus on individuals, homeowners. The
publicity from the grand opening of the Mor-Lang project
should generate some new clients. And in the meantime, I
have my income from Mor-Lang." Feeling better about her
financial future, she sat down on the arm of the chair and gave
Becca a squeeze. "How'd you get so smart?"

"I didn't. The solutions are all yours. Now, let's talk
about Chase."

Kate shot off the arm of the chair as if Becca had hit an eject button. She plopped down beside the pile of chocolate and began fishing for a Hershey's, avoiding her sister's gaze. "What about him?"

"Do you love him?"

"Yes. I mean, no." Kate's shoulders slumped. "Oh, I don't know what I mean. I love Chase Morgan, the repairman, not Chase Morgan the successful businessman."

"Aren't they one and the same?"

"Yes…no. Oh, I don't know," Kate said in frustration. "Can't you imagine the shock I felt when I discovered Chase was my employer? Although Joe told me he had a partner, I'd never met him, but I had a preconceived idea of what he'd be like. Fat, fifty and bald."

Kate pulled up her knees and nibbled at the chocolate bar. "And in the meantime, there was Chase, popping in and out of my house, preaching to me about trust and commitment. The entire time he was deceiving me, making me think he worked for my landlord, and keeping secret the fact that he was my employer." Woefully, she dropped her chin to her knees. "The heck of it is, in spite of everything he's done, I still love the man."

Becca tried to hide a smile. "Do you realize what you just said?"

Kate tipped up her face to meet Becca's knowing gaze. "What?"

Becca shrugged. "You said you loved him."

Kate stared at her sister a moment as the realization of what she'd unconsciously said soaked in. Knowing it was the truth, she dropped her forehead to her knees on a groan. "Oh, God. I accused him of lying to me. I even told him

our relationship in the future would be strictly business."
She lifted tear-filled eyes to Becca. "I think I really blew it
this time."

"I wouldn't throw in the towel yet. Give him a chance to
cool off, then call him. Tell him what you just told me."

Slowly, Kate rose to her feet. "Do you think he'll understand?"

"You'll never know until you try."

Kate heaved a deep breath, then smiled gratefully at her
sister. "Becca, you're a godsend." She held out a hand. "Come
on, little sister. I'll buy you a Fudgsicle."

Kate immediately put into action her plan to strengthen her
business. She spent hours working on the decorating sketches
for Mor-Lang's grand opening. Everything had to be perfect.
She'd accept no less.

Draperies were ordered. Subcontractors called and scheduled. Furniture and accessories ordered. Two weeks passed,
and Chase hadn't returned yet. She missed him and ached to
talk to him, but knew in her heart she would be wise to wait until
he returned from his trip before attempting a confrontation.

The only person she could think of who might have heard
from him was Joe Langford. Planning to fish for the information she wanted, Kate gave him a call.

"Joe? It's Kate."

"Please, no problems."

She laughed at the desperation in his voice. "No, no
problems. In fact, everything's going great! Everybody's lined
up to start next week. The painters will bring their crews in
on Monday morning. They'll finish in four days—that's a
promise. The paperhangers will work through the weekend.

And we should be ready for the carpet by Tuesday. I checked on the draperies today and they're nearly completed. Delivery on the furnishings are scheduled for Tuesday. That'll leave me with three days to get everything placed before the grand opening, but we can do it."

"Whew-ee! You've been busy."

"Yes, I have, but I've enjoyed every minute." Kate wrapped the telephone cord around her hand and tried to keep the tone of her voice neutral. "Have you heard from Chase?"

"Yeah. As a matter of fact, I talked to him this morning." Joe chuckled. "Have you seen him since he got back from Austin?"

"He's in Dallas?"

Joe's chuckles turned to roars of laughter. "Yeah, flew in this morning, and wait'll you see him!" He laughed again. "I just wish I could see the other guy."

"What other guy? Joe, you're talking in riddles."

Before Kate had a chance to question him further, Joe's secretary buzzed him. "Gotta go, Kate. I've got another call."

"What in the world is going on?" Kate exclaimed as she replaced the receiver. Then she realized what Joe had said—Chase was back in town. She grabbed her car keys and purse, knowing he'd be at the property site.

Twenty minutes later, she stopped her car at the main entrance. The security guard walked over as she rolled down her window.

"Hello, George. How's the head?"

He touched the bandage that still plastered his forehead. "Healing up fine, Miss McGinis. Just fine. Mr. Morgan's got people running all over this place getting ready for the grand opening. I believe we're going to make it," he beamed, obviously proud to be a part of the activities.

"Good! I'm going over to the models to check on progress there. See you later." She waved and accelerated her car.

Kate stopped on the paved street running in front of the three homes and admired them from a distance. The exterior painting was complete. The landscapers had sodded the front lawns with Saint Augustine grass and were busy planting evergreen shrubs and pansies in the bricked flower beds. Winding brick walkways led up the front entrance of each home.

Kate walked up to the first model whose two-story exterior looked as if it had been plucked straight out of the French countryside and planted in Dallas. When she entered, she noted the drywall was complete and followed the buzzing sound of a saw to the kitchen.

The carpenter switched off the motor when he saw Kate approach. "Hi, Kate. We're just about finished here."

She ran her hand along the smoothly sanded top of a cabinet door. "It looks great, Pete." She glanced around at the stacks of lumber and sawdust littering the floor. "Will you be finished by Monday morning?"

"Gone by Sunday. You can bank on that." He gave Kate a reassuring smile. "Most of this stuff is scraps. The boys are cleaning up the other models while I finish cutting the trim work for this one." He pulled a handkerchief from the back pocket of his overalls and wiped the sawdust from his face. "You need to go over to No. 3 and look at the desk you designed for the kitchen. It turned out real pretty."

Kate waved as he started up the saw and she walked over to No. 3. She went straight to the kitchen, and with a critical eye, studied the desk. The bottom portion consisted of two drawers on the left side with a cut-out area on the right for a chair. Slotted nooks for bills and mail lined the back of the desktop. Above this, a drawer stretched across the length of the desk. Its five-inch depth was planned to hold placemats and napkins. Kate had already purchased knickknacks and recipe books to fill the three shelves above the drawer. The highest shelf was a wine rack.

She pulled out the top desk drawer. The front portion of the drawer was divided into two three-by-five sections to hold recipe cards. The back would hold pencils, pens and other odd items. Closing it, she pulled out the bottom drawer. She'd designed it to hold file folders.

Satisfied with the carpenter's work on her sketches, she walked through the remainder of the house, double-checking each detail.

She was bending over the sunken tub in the master bath to pick up a stray piece of molding, when without warning she was grabbed from behind. A scream built in her throat, but was stifled as a strong hand clamped over her mouth.

"Don't scream. You'll have everyone on the property tearing in here," Chase warned in a gruff voice.

Kate peeled his fingers away from her mouth as she twirled to face him. "What are you trying to do?" she said, fighting for breath. "Scare me to death?"

"I thought I told you to never come out here by yourself."

"I'm not alone. I checked in with the security guard, and Pete is over in No. 1 working," she said, automatically taking a defensive stance.

"If I was able to come up behind you and grab you, don't you think a prowler could do the same?"

Kate heaved a deep breath. She was determined not to argue with him. He'd been gone almost two weeks, and those two weeks had seemed to her like two years. She wanted to talk to him. Civilly. Maturely. And that meant holding in her temper.

She sucked in another calming breath and released it, saying, "You're right." She glanced up and saw that his left eye was swollen and bruised a blue-green. So that's what Joe had meant when he'd asked her if she'd seen him. She forced back a smile. "Did *you* have a run-in with the prowler?"

Chase gingerly fingered his puffy eye. "No. Let's just say I was evening the score."

Kate clasped her hands behind her back. "If you evened it up, how'd the other guy look?"

"He may be drinking out of a straw for a while." He rubbed the back of his neck.

She noticed the weary gesture and the dark circle under his good eye. "Did you solve your problems in Austin?"

"I'm not sure yet, but I have a good idea who's causing them. Are you through here?"

"Yes. I only wanted to make sure the carpenters would be through so the painters could start first thing Monday."

"Good. I need a ride home. I had one of the boys pick me up at the airport this morning and drop me off here."

The drive home was a quiet one. Intent on navigating her way through the busy traffic on the LBJ, Kate didn't notice Chase had fallen asleep until she turned to ask him a question. His head rested on the back of the seat, his Stetson pulled down low over his eyes. His legs were stretched out in front of him as far as the car interior allowed.

She saved her question until she turned onto the street leading to her house. "Chase? Are you asleep?" she whispered cautiously.

"I was."

She winced. "Sorry, but I don't know where you live."

He rubbed his hand wearily across his eyes. "I was hoping to finagle an invitation for dinner from you."

"Are you hungry?"

"I usually am about this time of day. And especially since I haven't had lunch or breakfast."

"Poor boy," she said with a shake of her head. "Can I add this to my expense account?"

He sat up and straightened his hat as he remembered her threat that their relationship in the future would be all business. "Forget it," he grumbled.

"I was only teasing. I'll feed you. After all, if it weren't for you, I couldn't afford to eat."

Chase cocked his head and looked at her through narrowed eyes. "What's that supposed to mean?"

"It's a long story." She turned into her drive and parked by the side door. She leaned across the seat and kissed him on the cheek. With her hand resting on his shoulder, she let out a sigh. "I'll tell you after dinner. It's something you don't need to hear on an empty stomach."

They entered the kitchen through the side door, and Chase moved to stand behind Kate as she peered into the freezer.

"How about cream of broccoli soup and ham sandwiches?"

Chase looked over her shoulder at the well-stocked freezer. "You have enough food in there to feed an army."

She laughed. "I know. It's hard to cook for one person. I make a recipe, eat what I want and freeze the rest." She pointed to the labeled containers. "Spaghetti, lasagna, chili, chicken casserole. Take your pick."

"Soup and sandwiches sounds good to me." He yawned.

Kate pushed him toward the living room. "Finish your nap. I'll call you when it's ready."

She put the soup and ham in the microwave to thaw, and went into the breakfast room to set the table. The phone rang, and Kate raced back to the kitchen to answer it before it woke up Chase.

"Hello?" she said in a low voice, pushing open the swinging door and standing on tiptoe to see if Chase had awakened. A glimpse of the rhythmic rise and fall of his chest assured her he still slept.

"Kate! Hi, it's Laura."

"Laura!" Kate hadn't heard from her friend since they'd said their tearful goodbyes in Washington. Laura had been the one person who'd stood by Kate throughout her separation and divorce from Philip. "How are you?"

"I'm fine. Jonathan and I are at the airport and I had a few minutes between flights, so I thought I'd give you a call."

"I'm so glad you did. Are you coming or going?"

The question made Laura laugh just as Kate had known it would. Kate had always teased her friend that she and her husband traveled so much, they should sell the home Kate had so lavishly decorated for them and stay in a hotel.

"Going. Jonathan and I were in Austin on business. We went to a dinner party last night at Senator Wilson's home, and I couldn't resist calling you and getting the latest scoop."

"Drop the newspaper jargon, Laura. Remember? You retired from your job as a reporter when you married Jonathan."

"Old habits die hard. Speaking of newspapers, give me your address. I want to send you a copy of the Austin paper."

"Why do I need a copy of the Austin paper?"

"That's the scoop! Your ex was at the cocktail party. He'd had a few too many and when Lucy Bender asked him about you, he started carrying on about you having an affair with some ditch digger in Dallas."

Kate's hand closed over her mouth to smother a groan. She glanced at Chase's sleeping form on her sofa. And at the black eye.

"And then he slugged him."

"Who slugged who?"

"This cowboy slugged Philip. He walked up to him and said, 'This is for Kate,' and slapped him right across the face. Then he said, 'And this is from me' and decked him with a right hook to the jaw. When he bent down to help Philip up, Philip socked him in the eye. It was priceless!"

Kate pressed the heel of her hand to her forehead. So that's how Chase had gotten the black eye.

"A reporter was there to cover the party for the society section, but…" she said, laughing, "he lucked out and got front-page coverage for his story. Were you really married to that cowboy?"

"Yes."

"And…" Laura encouraged helpfully.

Kate pushed open the swinging door a crack and peeked through to the living room beyond. Her heart swelled at the sight of Chase sprawled on her sofa. "And I may just marry him again, if he'll have me."

Nine

Kate pushed through the swinging door and tiptoed to the living room. At the sofa, she knelt and laid a gentle finger to Chase's swollen eye, smiling tenderly. He flinched as her finger touched the bruised skin.

"Does it hurt?" she asked in concern.

Eyeing her suspiciously through the slit of his bruised and puffy eye, Chase mumbled, "Not much." He fitted his hands together into a fist over his head and stretched. "Actually, it looks worse than it feels." He scooted over to give Kate room to sit beside him on the sofa and reached for her hand.

"Why did you hit him?"

He froze, his hand just short of Kate's. Guiltily, he looked at her before twining his fingers through hers. "How'd you know?"

"A friend of mine called while you were sleeping. She was at the party."

He dropped his gaze to his thumb where it rubbed slowly up and down the length of hers. "I'm sorry you found out. I'd hoped you wouldn't."

"Why?"

"I figured it'd make you mad. And you were mad enough at me when I left."

"Mad?" Kate asked in surprise. "I wish I'd had the nerve to do it myself. He's had it coming for a long time." She laughed as she pictured the very cool and proper Philip sprawled on the floor.

Chase shook his head, frowning. "You don't understand. It was a bad scene. A photographer snapped a picture just as I threw a punch. We made the headlines. Chivalry Still Alive In Texas, with a subheading Cowboy Fights For Lady's Honor. It looked like something straight out of the *National Intruder.*"

He took a deep breath, stalling for time, while he steeled himself for the explosion that was sure to come once Kate heard the rest of the story. "The reporter obviously saw an opportunity to get his byline on the front page because he did some digging and found out you and I were once married. Now all of Texas knows our sordid past."

Chase expected anything and everything—kicking, screaming, cursing—and was prepared to stand and take whatever blows came his way. He was knocked senseless when she simply leaned over, placed her hands on his cheeks and kissed him tenderly on the mouth. "I don't care," she murmured against his lips. "I think you're the most wonderful man in the whole world." She touched a finger to the end of his nose. "But you might be sorry you slugged him."

"Why's that?"

"Philip doesn't like to be made a fool of. And he's vindictive. I've learned the hard way to never turn my back on him."

"I don't see why he'd feel the need for revenge." He touched his swollen, blue-green eye. "He got his punch in."

"That wouldn't be enough for Philip. Remember the night you met him over here?"

"Yeah," he replied dryly, remembering the evening all too well.

"After you left, he said some pretty rotten things about you. When I defended you, it only angered him more."

Chase tried hard to suppress the glimmer of pleasure that spread through his chest. "You defended me?"

"Yes. And he said I'd regret what I said. But no matter what else he can concoct with that devious mind of his, I don't regret a word."

Chase tensed, his hand tightening on hers. "Has he hurt you?"

"Not physically. And I'm not sure he's done anything, really, but all of a sudden my work here has dried up to nothing—except for the Mor-Lang project—just like it did in Washington after we divorced. And earlier this week my attorney called to tell me there's been a delay in the property settlement from my divorce."

"Is that what you meant when you said if it weren't for me you wouldn't be eating?"

"Yes," she said, chuckling, then added, "But it's not really that bad, yet." Kate looked into his eyes, the laughter fading from her eyes. "Be careful, Chase. He plays dirty."

Chase released Kate's hand and threaded his fingers together behind his head, annoyance twisting one side of his mouth. "I think I've already discovered how dirty he can play. Unless I miss my guess, he was my problem on the renovation project. Some legislators in Austin have been nosing around, trying to find ways to delay our construction schedule. Time is money and every delay they've caused has cost me a bundle."

A sick feeling tightened Kate's stomach as she listened, remembering her conversation with her father in the garden. She'd all but thrown in his face the fact that she loved Chase and was seeing him again. Jack McGinis had more friends in Austin, Texas, than Philip Michels ever hoped to have. She placed a warning hand on Chase's chest. "Philip may not be your problem. It may be my dad."

Chase cut his eyes toward her. "Your dad?"

Kate swallowed back the nausea that rose in her throat, regretting flaunting her relationship with Chase under her father's nose. More than anything in the world, she wanted to be with Chase…but not if their being together destroyed him. She balled her hands into tight fists in her lap, guilt overriding her own selfish emotions. "Maybe it'd be better if I quit working for you and didn't see you anymore. Then Dad wouldn't be gunning for you, and Philip wouldn't have reason to cause you trouble."

Slowly, Chase pulled his hands from behind his head. He pried her hands apart and clasped them in his own. "No way, lady," he said, his voice firm as he pulled her down beside him. "I can handle your father and I can handle Philip Michels, but what I can't handle is being away from you." He pressed his lips to hers. "I missed you, Kate." His voice was husky and heavy with emotion. His mouth touched hers again and a small flame spread through Kate's abdomen.

She leaned back and touched a corner of his mouth with the ball of her thumb. "I missed you, too, Chase. But are you sure our being together is worth all the trouble they might cause you?"

"Positive."

Comforted by his assurance, but not at all sure he was making the right decision, she snuggled against his shoulder. "Have you forgiven me for the way I acted when I discovered you were my landlord and my boss?"

He nipped at her thumb with his teeth. "There's nothing to forgive. I don't blame you for being mad."

If he'd said he'd forgiven her, Kate might very well have come off the sofa raving, for although she did regret her actions, she felt they were justified. She'd spent most of her life being manipulated—first by her father, then by Philip—and had vowed that no man would ever have that level of control over her again. Chase's sharing in the responsibility of their quarrel let her know that he understood that. Relieved, she relaxed against him with a sigh.

Her gaze settled on his feet hanging over the edge of the sofa. "Did you know I have a bed in this house?"

He buried his nose in the auburn hair covering her ear. "Are you bragging, or is that an invitation?"

"I just thought since all of Texas is probably talking about us right now, maybe we should give them something to talk about."

Air whooshed out of Kate's lungs as Chase rolled over her and stood. He scooped her up into his arms and loped down the hallway to the master bedroom, with Kate laughing as she bounced against his chest. He pushed the door open with the toe of his boot, crossed the room in three long strides and jumped onto the brass bed with Kate still in his arms.

She squealed as she landed hard against Chase's firm body. Laughing, she wrapped her arms around his neck. "Have I ever told you how much I love you?"

His body stilled, and Kate watched the expression on his

face turn from laughter to something akin to disbelief. "Say that again."

Her gaze met his and locked, her voice a soft whisper. "I love—" His lips absorbed the rest of the phrase as they found hers, not allowing himself to believe her, but moved by the words nonetheless.

He rose to his knees, pulling Kate up, as well, until she knelt on the bed in front of him, her body pressed close to his. His hands drifted down her sides, his fingers catching the hem of her sweater. With a gentle tug, he pulled upward, the sweater forcing their lips apart. He tugged higher, trapping her arms in the soft folds of her sweater above her head.

He rocked back on his heels, and she felt his gaze burning into her skin; then he leaned into her and placed his lips in the valley between her breasts.

She melted against him, cradling his head between cashmere-covered hands. He moaned her name, and the skin beneath his lips sizzled at the touch. At once hot and frustrated, she struggled free of the confining sweater that impeded her movements and tossed it in a crumpled heap on the floor.

Aching to touch Chase, she tugged his shirt free of his slacks, then she undid the last pearlized snap and ran her knuckles up the front of his shirt. His chest lay bare before her, and she splayed her hands across it, pushing him back onto the pillow at the head of the bed. Her lips sought his, allowing him to taste the fire burning within her.

How he'd missed her. This is what he wanted. This is what he needed. This is what had been missing from his life. If he had to fight Jack McGinis and Philip Michels every step of the way, he intended to have Kate McGinis. His fingers found the clasp of her bra and freed it, then tossed it to the floor. With an impatient groan, he pressed her to him, gently rubbing her breasts against the coarse hair on his chest. They clung to each other, reveling in the heady sensation.

Impatient and greedy, Kate unhooked the Western buckle at his waist and pulled the belt through the loops of his slacks. Her fingers sought first the hook, then the zipper tab. In her haste to strip him, her knuckles rubbed against the fullness of his desire as she eased the zipper down.

A guttural groan came from deep in Chase's throat. He rolled, pinning her beneath him with her arms stretched above her head. He held her there with hands strong enough to snap the slender bones of her wrists. Captive, Kate surrendered to the savage assault of his lips as he nipped and plunged in his attempt to consume her. His hands continued to bind her wrists as he trailed his lips down her face, over the edge of her chin, dropping to her neck, then coursing farther down to settle at her breast. He nibbled at each rose-colored bud, teasing Kate until she was writhing beneath him, crazy with need.

"Chase, please." She strained against the hands that held hers. She wanted to be free. Free to touch him, hold him, love him.

"Not yet, Kate." With each word, his breath fanned hot against her skin. He traced a line from her breasts to her navel with his tongue while his hands slid from her wrists to her elbows. The crisp cotton sheets burned her skin as he forced her arms to her sides.

A strand of fire, scalding hot, twisted through her when his lips found the soft skin of her inner thigh. Her hips arched up, demanding more than just the artful pleasure of his tongue.

Unable to hold back any longer, Chase rose to his knees and pulled Kate's legs to wrap around his waist. With a single thrust, he plunged into her.

Rockets exploded, sending shock waves ricocheting through Kate. Her body convulsed, her hips arching to meet each driving thrust, matching his rhythm with a demanding one of her own. She soared higher and higher, seeking that utmost peak of satisfaction. She gasped when at last she reached it, crying out his name, clinging to him as she hung at the crest. She tumbled over the edge as answering shudders racked Chase's body. She floated downward through a sultry haze of the most exquisite pleasure she had ever known.

A fine mist of perspiration covered Chase's body as he held Kate, his chest heaving with each breath. Without releasing his hold on her, he turned until they both lay on their sides facing each other. His fingers traced the curves of her body from the swell of her breasts, down the gentle slope of her waist, to her hips.

"You're beautiful," he whispered, closing his eyes against the sight of her nudity, a vision so beautiful it hurt him just to behold. He pulled her to him. "And you're mine."

She nestled closer, lying cheek to chest, stomach to groin and thigh to knee. Dinner was forgotten, for Kate had satisfied a far deeper hunger within Chase. When the perspiration on his body began to cool, he pulled up the sheet and blanket to cover them. Kate snuggled closer and slept.

Morning brought sunshine streaming across the patio and through the French doors, bathing the sleeping lovers in a rich, golden glow.

The phone rang, piercing the early morning quiet.

Chase's hand batted at the nightstand until his fingers settled on the receiver. "Hello?" he grumbled sleepily into the mouthpiece.

"I'm sorry. I must have the wrong number," a woman's voice offered in apology. "I was calling Kate McGinis."

Chase groaned and prodded Kate with the receiver. "I think it's your mother," he whispered in embarrassment.

Kate grabbed the phone and sat up, instantly awake. "Good morning, Mom."

"Kate? Is that you?"

"Yes, it's me." She smothered a giggle as she watched Chase bury his head under the pillow.

"Who answered the phone?"

"Chase."

There was a pregnant pause before her mother spoke again, her voice tinged with amusement. "It sounded like I woke him."

"You did. But that's okay. How are you?"

"I'm fine. How are *you?*"

Kate rested her back against the headboard and stretched like a cat drunk on cream. "Fine. Just fine."

"When I talked to Becca last night, she seemed to be worried about you, but it appears you have everything under control."

Kate reached over, lifted the edge of Chase's pillow and looked at him. Her breath whispered out on a satisfied sigh. "Yes, everything is fine now."

"Kate, I don't want to sound like an interfering mother, but do me a favor. Tell that man to marry you. And stay that way this time."

Kate tossed back her head and laughed. "Okay, Mom. I will. I'll call you back later."

She leaned across Chase, placing a palm on the constricted muscles on his back for balance as she stretched to replace the receiver in the phone cradle. He peeked out from underneath the pillow. "What did she say?"

Kate slanted her face to his and in a serious tone, whis pered, "She said you should marry me."

He disappeared under the pillow with a groan. "I can't believe I answered the phone."

Kate flopped back against the headboard and crossed her arms in mock indignation. "Does this mean you don't intend to marry me?"

His arm snaked out and pulled Kate under the pillow with him. "No," he said in frustration. "It means I'm embarrassed because I got caught in bed with Mrs. McGinis's daughter."

His hand pressed against Kate's cheek, forcing her gaze to meet his. "Do you think she'd believe you if you told her nothing happened? That I just slept here?"

"Probably not."

"In that case," he said before finding her lips, then mumbling into them, "something's definitely going to happen!"

He threw off the pillow and pulled Kate on top of him, her naked body fitting flush against his. Desire pulsed through him, hardening him instantly to an aching readiness as he clasped the cheeks of her buttocks in his hands. When he looked into Kate's eyes, he was nearly blinded by the passion- ate heat he found there. Groaning, he closed his eyes and took her with a savageness, a wildness that matched the need raging within him.

With the promise of dinner and a tour of his home, Kate followed Chase through the back door of his house. Skidding to a stop on the sawdust-covered floor, she tried hard to suppress the gasp of shock that immediately welled in her throat. Pressing her fingers tight over her lips, she glanced around the room, her eyes widening in disbelief, at the sight that greeted her.

Piles of debris were heaped everywhere and a fine dusting of white powder covered it all. The wall opposite her was three-quarters demolished, offering a distorted view of a breakfast room between bared studs and a torn wallboard. Fragments of the broken wallboard were scattered about the floor and electrical wiring dangled exposed and dangerous between two-by-four studs riddled with nails.

If that weren't enough to throw Kate into a tailspin, lumber and plumbing supplies were stacked in the living room just visible through a doorway void of a door. There wasn't a stick of furniture in sight.

Chase kicked at empty paint cans and litter to clear a path to the breakfast bar. Once there, with one fell swoop of his forearm across the tile surface, he sent paintbrushes, tools and other paraphernalia flying. After setting the sack of food on the counter, he turned to Kate, grinning, "Well, this is it! My humble abode."

Kate tried hard to return his smile, but finally gave up. Her lips compressed in a thin line, she marched across the room to stand beside him. "You *live* here?" she demanded to know.

He turned back to the bar and opened the sack, pulling out a grease-stained box of fried chicken. "Yep."

Kate thought she detected a measure of pride in the clipped, one-syllable response, but where it came from she couldn't imagine. She glanced through horror-filled eyes around her. "For how long?"

"'Bout three months. As soon as I finished up the remodeling on the house you're living in, I moved on to this one."

Suspicion dawned as Kate lifted her gaze to stare at his profile. Chase had always loved working with wood and restoring old things. He'd often told her a living could be made doing just that. It appeared he'd been living out his dream for the past seven years—if you could call living amongst all this rubble, living—while she had lived in the lap of luxury. The contrast made her heart twist violently in her chest. "And you stayed in my house while you worked on it?"

"Yep, although the house on Kenwood wasn't in as bad a shape as this one when I started on it." He eyed the partially demolished wall and gestured at it with a plastic container. "The wiring and plumbing all need to be replaced, which will take some time and a chunk of money, but the end results will be well worth the effort."

"How long have you been doing this?"

Chase cut a glance at her. "Remodeling?" At her slow nod, he explained. "I bought the first house a couple of months after our divorce. I lived there until I had it ready to sell, sold it and used the profits to buy another one. All told, I've restored nine houses and own three others that are leased out at the moment because I haven't had time to work on them." He placed the container of coleslaw on the countertop and reached into the sack for the baked beans. "I used the profits from my remodeling business to buy into a partnership with Joe on the subdivision. If all goes well, by the time the lots all sell, I'll be a rich man." He set the container of baked beans next to the coleslaw and turned to face Kate. "After we eat, I'll give you the grand tour."

Kate snatched up the coleslaw and beans and stuffed them right back into the gaping sack. "The tour can wait." Her hand shook as she grabbed the box of chicken. "Right now, you're moving."

Chase planted a hand over hers, stilling her agitated movements. "Whoa! Just a minute. Says who?"

"Says me." She shook off his hand and dropped the box into the sack. Wadding the sack closed in one fist, she lifted her chin and narrowed her eyes, daring him to disagree. "From this moment forward, you are living with me." She took a deep breath, clutching the sack at her waist. "Now," she said, fighting for calm, "show me your bedroom and I'll help you pack."

Chase stared at her, his eyes growing darker and darker with each passing second. He snatched the sack from her grasp and slammed it back down on the counter. "And just exactly what is wrong with where I currently live?"

"Nothing." Kate brushed at the tears that welled in her eyes, not wanting him to see them and mistake them for pity. "It's just that—" Emotion clotted her throat, making any further explanation all but impossible. She pressed trembling fingers against her lips, breathing deeply in an attempt to rein in her galloping emotions. "You need a home," she finally managed, and turned away from him. "You *deserve* a home. A place with furniture and a clean floor." She kicked at a stray piece of wallboard at her feet. "And a wall to hang pictures on," she cried, her voice rising hysterically as she watched the wallboard sail through a gap in the kitchen wall. She covered her face with her hands, then ripped them off to wheel and face him. "Why do you live like this, Chase?"

Slowly, he sank down onto an upended crate he frequently used for a chair, his gaze riveted on Kate's face. He'd seen her angry before. A few of those times the anger had been directed at him. But this was different, he felt the difference well from deep in his gut. She wasn't mad *at* him. She was mad *for* him, and the anger had to be because she cared. But there was something else behind the anger. Something he couldn't quite put a finger on.

"Habit, I guess," he said slowly, still watching her. "The first house I bought, I didn't have a choice but to live there while I worked on it. I didn't have the money to live anywhere else." He lifted his hands in a futile gesture, then dropped them to his knees. "After I sold the place and proved to myself I could make a living doing work I loved, I guess I got greedy…or maybe just complacent." He shook his head as he rose to his feet, uncomfortable with this analysis. He dug his fingers through his hair as he paced away. "Hell! I don't know. I just kept living like this, socking away every penny I could and reinvesting it in real estate."

Though his words and the look of discomfort on his face tore at Kate's heart, she held firm, not allowing herself to go to him. "But why, Chase? Why? Was making money that important to you?"

"Hell, yes, it was important!" he roared back at her. "Not having any was the reason I lost you and I was determined never to be caught in that position again. I had to prove that I—" he jabbed his thumb at his chest "—could be just as successful as your old man."

"Prove to who?" she asked quietly.

The question made him stop and stare. Who was he trying to prove his worthiness to? Himself? Nah, he thought, and mentally shoved away the ridiculous notion. Money didn't mean anything to him. Never had. He glanced around. Surely the bleakness and the simplicity of his existence was proof enough of that.

"Did you want to prove something to me?"

The question had Chase whipping his gaze back to Kate. Anger heated his blood and sent it racing through his veins. "Maybe," he replied curtly.

"You don't have to, you know," she said, taking a step toward him. "Seven years ago, I married you because I loved you, not because of your net worth." When she reached him, she stopped and lifted her gaze to his. "Do you believe me now, Chase, when I say I love you?"

Chase stared at her, his body trembling as he forced himself to focus on the gold flecks within the sea of green. He wanted to believe her. God, how he wanted to believe. But seven years ago he'd believed and nearly lost his mind when she'd left.

He turned away, his jaw set and unforgiving. "I don't know."

Kate closed her eyes and sucked in a deep breath. She opened them to stare at his unrelenting back. She'd lived seven years not knowing if he loved her or not, and she hadn't come this far in the process of dealing with her past to walk away just because Chase Morgan was incapable or unwilling to share his emotions and feelings with her.

Slowly, she closed the distance he'd put between them. She placed a hand in the narrow valley between his shoulder blades. He flinched at the touch, but she refused to remove her hand. "I understand, Chase. Really, I do. And it doesn't matter, because this time I'm not running away. I'm going to prove to you that you can trust me again."

Ten

Kate headed down the drive with tears stinging her eyes. She wanted to cry, but refused to allow herself the childish display of emotion. She feared if she started, she'd never be able to stop. Instead she concentrated on putting one foot in front of the other, carrying herself farther and farther away from Chase's house.

He'll come after me, she told herself. I know he will. He's just being stubborn because he has such a hard time trusting people. Once he thinks about what I said, he'll realize I'm sincere. With each step she took, she listened, straining to hear the slam of a door and the reassuring scrape of boot heels hurrying on the sidewalk behind her.

After walking a full block with nothing but the sound of an occasional dog barking and the crunch of dried leaves under her own feet, she quit listening.

He wasn't coming after her.

The thought saddened Kate, but she squared her shoulders and lifted her chin, blinking back the sting of disappointment. She wouldn't give up on him, although she fully believed that's what he expected her to do. She'd promised him that she wouldn't run away, that she'd prove he could trust her, and that's exactly what she intended to do.

One way or another, she'd prove to him that Kate McGinis was no quitter.

Jack McGinis glanced up from the papers spread across his desk. When he saw Kate, his lips thinned in disgust. "I told your mother I didn't want to be disturbed."

There was a time in her life when the verbal snub would have sent Kate scurrying for cover. But not now. She angled a wing-back chair in front of the desk and sat down. "I know. She told me. But I needed to talk to you."

His eyes narrowed suspiciously. "About what?"

"About Mor-Lang Properties." Kate watched her father's face, waiting to see if the mention of Chase's company drew any response. Oddly, his face remained expressionless.

"What the devil is Mor-Lang?" he asked as he shuffled papers, obviously irritated to have his work disturbed and anxious to get back to it.

"One of Chase's companies."

"So?"

"Mor-Lang owns a tract of land just north of town where they are developing a new subdivision. Chase is also involved in a restoration project on a city block in downtown Dallas." She waited for a reaction. When none was forthcoming, she pressed on. "Because the city block includes an historical landmark, Chase is having to deal with several government agencies, on local, state and federal levels."

Her father fell back against his chair, snatching his reading glasses from his face. "What in tarnation does all this have to do with me?"

"I'm not sure."

He leaned an elbow on his desk and aimed his glasses at her. "If you're wanting me to pull some strings to benefit Chase Morgan, young lady, you can damn well forget it. I wouldn't spit on the man if he were on fire." He shoved the glasses back onto his nose and dragged the papers in front of him.

Kate stood and leaned over the desk, planting a hand on the papers her father studied, forcing him to look at her. "I'm not asking you to do anything to help Chase," she said, her voice low, but level. "I'm simply asking that you don't do anything to hurt him, either."

Not waiting for a reaction this time, she spun on her heels and marched from her father's study, silently applauding her first step in winning Chase's trust. Now for step two.

The phone rang, but Chase ignored it, continuing to hammer wallboard into place. On the fourth ring, the answering machine clicked on and his own voice filled the room.

He lowered the hammer and popped three more nails between his lips.

"Chase? Are you there?"

At the sound of Kate's voice, he straightened and looked at the machine, frowning.

"Oh, well, it's Kate. Sorry I missed you. It's seven o'clock and I just made lasagna and a salad and thought you might like to come over for dinner. If you get home and are hungry, come on over. I'll be up late working on some silk floral arrangements I'm making for the models. Love you." Click.

Gritting his teeth, Chase walked to the breakfast bar, punched the erase button and reset the machine. It was an act. He could tell by the overly cheerful tone of her voice. She thought she could be sweet as sugar, pretend that nothing was wrong and all their problems would miraculously disappear.

He didn't know what kind of game Kate was playing this time, but he sure as hell wasn't going to play along.

He'd played the sucker once for her. Never again.

Kate stumbled into the kitchen, still feeling a bit green around the gills. She'd stayed up late, working on the floral arrangements and hoping Chase would respond to her invitation for dinner. He hadn't, and in the wee hours of the morning she'd finally dumped the lasagna in the sink and gone to bed. After a few hours' sleep, she'd awakened, feeling nauseous, and spent a good thirty minutes in the bathroom, hugging the toilet.

A cup of weak tea and a cracker, she told herself, remembering her mother's cure for an upset stomach. She stumbled on to the pantry, nabbed a tea bag and a tin of crackers and made her way to the sink. After pulling a mug from the cupboard, she leaned to turn on the tap. The plate of leftover lasagna stared up at her from the bottom of the sink. The sight of the greasy, sauce-encrusted noodles made her stomach roll. At the same moment water from the tap hit the plate and sent the spicy scent of tomatoes and garlic shooting just beneath her nose.

With her hand clamped tight over her mouth, Kate wheeled and ran for the guest bath down the hall.

* * *

"Hi, guys!" Kate waltzed through the back door, wearing a bright smile and juggling a basket filled with a colorful assortment of silk vegetables and eucalyptus. After an hour of gut-wrenching heaves, finally she had something to smile about. Her stomach was back in place and she was beginning to feel almost human again.

She plunked the basket on the center of the pine table, arranged a plaid runner underneath it, and stepped back to admire her work. She glanced over her shoulder to look at Chase and Joe, who were in the kitchen hanging a light fixture. Both seemed oblivious to her presence. "Well, what do you think?"

Joe stepped from the ladder. "Looks good to me." He glanced at Chase. "What do you think?"

Without looking at Kate or the arrangement, Chase grunted an unintelligible response and folded the ladder. Gathering it under his arm, he headed for the back door, slamming it behind him.

Kate fought to keep her smile in place.

Joe didn't even try. He scowled at the back door where his partner had just exited. "I don't know what's gotten in to him this morning, Kate. He's grumpy as an old bear. Do you want me to knock some sense into him for you?"

Kate sucked in a deep breath and calmly smoothed her hands down her thighs. "No, I'd like the privilege of doing that myself." She marched to the back door. "But thanks for the offer, Joe," she said, then slammed the door with the same force Chase had only moments before.

She caught sight of him at the rear of his truck, angling the ladder onto the truck bed. Firming her lips, she headed for him. "Chase. I'd like a word with you."

He lifted the lid on his toolbox, refusing to look at her. "What about?"

"About your attitude." When he continued to fiddle with tools in his toolbox, Kate caught his elbow and jerked him around. "I know you don't trust me, and considering everything, I guess I can understand that. But how in the world am I supposed to *prove* you can trust me, when you won't talk to me, you won't return my phone calls and every time I enter a room, you exit it?"

Chase pulled his elbow from her grip and turned back to the toolbox. "You've got an overactive imagination. I'm just busy."

"Too busy to return a phone call, to drop by my house? Too busy to say I love you, Kate?"

Chase wheeled, his eyes shooting fire. He grabbed Kate by the shoulders, squeezing until she winced at the pain. "I don't know what kind of game you're playing, but count me out." He snatched his hands from her and whirled back to his truck.

"This is no game, Chase." She moved around him until she could stare at his profile. "I love you, and I'm not going to give up until you can say you *don't* love me." She drew closer still. "Can you say that, Chase? Can you say you don't love me? Can you?" she persisted.

He whipped his head around to glare at her. Though his lips trembled and the words seemed to pulse at his throat, not a sound passed his lips. Finally, he whirled around and stomped off, leaving her standing beside his truck.

From the inside of the model home, the windows seemed to be painted black, a result of the inky night beyond. Every light in the house was ablaze, turning the windows into a dark screen that reflected different angles of the room's interior on the glass panes, depending on where a person stood. The time was nearly midnight, the day before the grand opening. The past week had been jam-packed and exhausting for everyone involved in the Mor-Lang project, but everything was at last in place.

Kate stepped down from the ladder and rubbed a weary hand at the ache in the small of her back, eyeing the picture she'd just hung.

"How's it going?"

Kate turned her head, finding a smile as she saw Joe enter the living room. "It's going," she replied dryly, chuckling. "How are things over at No. 4?"

"The decorator is hanging the drapes," Joe said, "and everything seems to be in order. Where's Chase?"

Kate pursed her lips. "Everywhere but where I am."

"I know it's none of my business, but what's going on between you two?"

She heaved a weary sigh. "I wish I knew." She sighed again, then managed a small smile for Joe. "But at the moment, I'm more concerned with getting this house ready for the grand opening tomorrow."

"Need any help?"

"As a matter of fact, I do." Kate gestured toward the sofa, which was sitting in the middle of the floor. "Now that the pictures are hung, we can move this back into place." She crossed to the far end of the sofa and stooped to gain a handhold on its base. "On the count of three. One…two…three." Kate lifted, straining under the sofa's weight. Walking stiff-legged, she groaned and grunted as she angled the sofa toward the wall, with Joe leading the way from the opposite end. "That's good," she said, huffing for breath.

Wiping the perspiration from her brow, she straightened…and felt the floor pitch beneath her feet. As darkness threatened, she grabbed for the wall, searching for something solid to sink her fingernails into.

"Joe?" she called, her voice weak and sounding as if it were coming from a million miles away. Before he could answer, her knees buckled and she folded, slamming her head against the wall as she fell.

Kate wasn't sure how long she was unconscious, but when she opened her eyes, Joe was kneeling over her, chafing her hand between his, his brow puckered in concern. "Are you okay?" he asked, his voice shaking.

"Yes." Kate pushed to one elbow and grimaced when a pain shot down the back of her neck. She lifted a hand to her head and felt the swell of a lump. "At least, I think I am."

"I'll get Chase." Joe started to rise, but Kate grabbed for his hand, stopping him.

"No. Please."

"But—"

"No, Joe," she said, making her voice firm. "I don't want you to get Chase. I don't even want you to tell Chase I fainted. He's got enough on his mind without having to worry about me."

The fainting spell troubled Kate more than she was willing to admit, for in addition to it, the nausea she'd experienced earlier in the week had persisted. Not one who experienced illness often, Kate blamed the odd maladies on nerves. And no wonder.

The deadline for completing the models for the grand opening had ticked like a time bomb set just out of reach. To add to her level of stress, she saw Chase daily at the subdivision, and he avoided her like the plague. She found that particular situation a hundred times more stressful than the deadline.

Her pledge not to leave Chase and to win back his trust seemingly had had no affect on him, for he hadn't spoken three words to her since she'd demanded he tell her he didn't love her. His attitude toward her was cool and reserved. His silent presence scraped on Kate's raw nerves like a dull saw on metal.

From the window of the first model, Kate watched the entrance with butterflies flapping in her stomach. Cars stretched a good half mile from the bricked entrance to the subdivision. A policeman stood in the midst, directing the snarl of traffic. In less than fifteen minutes, the scrolled gates would be opened and the public would be invited in.

At the moment Kate was alone. Joe and Chase were holding court in the tract office, cutting deals with builders on the remaining vacant lots. Mrs. Kimbrough and Rhonda, Joe's wife, and other Mor-Lang employees were strategically placed throughout the models to answer questions and guide interested parties to the sales office if needed.

Kate both needed and hated the solitude. For the past week, she had pushed herself physically and mentally to see that her portion of the responsibilities were met. Ads had been placed in the newspapers, spots run on local radio stations. At Kate's request, a television crew had even come out and done a short segment, giving their viewers a glimpse of Dallas's hottest new subdivision and the model Kate had decorated with a country theme.

Chase had remained just off camera while Kate had led the crew through the home. She had smiled and talked to the cameras and the television show's engaging host, but inside she was dying, wondering if Chase would ever find the nerve to declare his love for her.

She sighed as she turned away from the window, telling herself that when the grand opening was over, she was going to demand an answer from him once and for all.

"Monday at four will be great for me." After making the notation, Kate replaced her appointment book and offered her hand to the young couple. "In the meantime, make a list of what you'd like done and arrive at a budget for us to work within."

"We don't have much money…" the woman began.

Though her feet ached and her smile felt like a crack in dried cement after three hours of greeting visitors to the model, Kate waved away the woman's uncertainties. "Don't worry. Decorating on a shoestring budget is my specialty."

The look of relief on the face of the young woman's husband warmed Kate's heart and almost made her laugh.

"Are there any vacant lots available?"

Kate waved to the young couple as they left before turning to answer the question directed her way. "Yes, the owners of the property are at the main office by the front gate. They have a plat map that shows all the remaining lots, which I'm sure they'd be happy to show you."

The front door opened for the thousandth time that day and Kate glanced up. Her smile broadened and her eyes lit up when she saw Becca. She waved her hand at her sister and brother-in-law, motioning them to join her. Her smile faded when they stepped across the threshold, revealing the couple behind them.

Kate felt the blood drain from her face and the starch from her knees. "Daddy," she whispered through fingers pressed tight against her lips.

* * *

Joe closed the plat book and reared back in his chair, scraping his hair from his forehead. He laced his hands behind his head and, with the toe of a boot, swiveled his chair around to face the rear of the office. Chase stood at the window, hands on his hips, staring at something or nothing, Joe couldn't tell which. But he knew Chase well enough to know by the angry set of his jaw that something was troubling his friend.

He pushed to his feet and crossed to stand behind Chase, peering over his partner's shoulder, taking a wild stab in the direction he figured his friend's mind was traveling. "She did a good job, didn't she?"

Lost in thought, Chase jerked at the unexpected closeness of Joe's voice. He glanced over his shoulder, frowned, then turned back to the window. "Who?"

Joe bit back a smile. If Chase had said "Yeah, she did," Joe would have fallen over backward in a swoon, because it would have been an acknowledgment from Chase of the fact that he was thinking about Kate. Because he hadn't, Joe knew without a doubt he was right on target. Chase was that stubborn.

"Kate. Just look at that crowd."

Chase did and his frown deepened. The crowd was there, all right, and, though he resented doing so, he had to give a lot of the credit to Kate. She had worked her butt off, getting the houses ready and contacting the media, ensuring the grand opening a large turnout…and driving him more than a little crazy in the process.

For a solid week she'd moved around him with a calmness, a sugar-sweet smile, a nothing-has-changed-in-our-relationship attitude that had Chase grinding his teeth. She was hell-bent on proving to him he could trust her, but he was wise to her methods. It was all an act, a facade that he could see through as clearly as he could see through the pane of glass in front of him.

He didn't know what she hoped to achieve if he told her that he loved her and trusted her…and he didn't plan on playing along with her little game long enough to find out. The pain just wasn't worth it.

Or so he tried to tell himself as he stared at the model home where he knew she was serving as hostess.

"I hope we haven't worked her too hard. She's a ball of energy, but she's fragile."

Chase almost laughed. Kate, fragile? "She's a big girl. She can take care of herself."

"I don't know," Joe said, shaking his head as he turned back to his desk. "She scared the hell out of me last night when she passed out."

Chase whipped around, his shoulders tensed and his eyes blazing. "She *what?*"

Joe took a nervous step backward at the lethal look in Chase's eye, knowing he'd broken a confidence to Kate, but sure that he was doing the right thing. "Passed out. We were moving the sofa and she just—"

Though Joe stood a head taller and outweighed Chase by a good forty pounds, Chase grabbed him by the knot of his tie and shoved him up against the wall. "What in the hell do you mean by letting her move furniture around? She's a woman, for God's sake! What do we pay all these big, strapping men around here for, anyway?"

"Now, wait a minute, Chase. You—"

"No, *you* wait a minute." He tightened his fingers on Joe's tie and watched his friend's face turn a deeper shade of red. "Why didn't you tell me Kate fainted?"

"She made me promise I wouldn't. Said she didn't want you worrying about her."

Chase's fingers went lax on Joe's tie. "She said that?"

Able to breathe freely again, Joe stuck a finger behind his tie and worked it loose, easing out a long, relieved breath. "Yeah. She said you had enough on your mind without having to worry about her."

Chase closed his eyes, tipping back his head and dropping his hands into tight fists at his sides. He stood there a minute, his body trembling, his face racked with emotion. Then suddenly he turned and, without a word, stormed out the back door.

Joe crossed to the window and peered out, still working his finger between his shirt and his neck. He watched Chase stalk across the vacant lot to the street behind the office that led to the first model. A smile slowly built on his face.

"Doesn't want to worry me, huh?" Chase mumbled angrily. He ignored the curious stares he received on the street from visitors moving from house to house. He stomped past them with one goal in mind. To reach Kate and give her the dressing down she deserved, then he was going to make her go home and go to bed, even if he had to bodily make her do it.

He jerked open the back door of the model, brushed past a group of people standing in the kitchen and pushed his way to the breakfast room.

He saw her standing not ten feet away, her hands pressed to her mouth, her shoulders shaking. Was she laughing? Crying? While he watched, trying to determine which, she crumpled. Like a rag doll who'd been dropped, she sagged to the floor in a heap.

Chase's heart rammed against his chest wall. "Kate!" He shouldered his way through the crowd of people separating him from her. When he reached her, he fell to one knee, brushing her hair back from her face with one hand while catching her wrist in the other.

A hand clamped his shoulder and pushed him aside, throwing him off balance.

"Call an ambulance," the man roared as he took Chase's place at Kate's side. "Everybody get back. Give her some room to breathe."

Kate's eyes blinked open. She looked up and a weak smile curved at her lips. "Daddy," she whispered. "I can't believe you're here."

His lips pursed, he tried hard to make his face stern. "Well, certainly I'm here. Couldn't miss my daughter's grand opening, now, could I?" He squeezed her hand in his. Kate noticed the slight tremble in his fingers and tears sprang to her eyes. "Now, you don't worry about a thing," he assured her, his voice gruff with emotion. "We've called an ambulance, and I'll take care of everything."

Kate caught a slight movement out of the corner of her eye and glanced up. Chase stood behind her father, his face expressionless, his eyes guarded but watchful. The very sight of him made fresh tears well in her eyes. She searched his face for some sign, some type of emotion to tell her he loved her and he cared for her, but found nothing. She looked at him a moment longer, then turned her gaze back to her father and did what she should have done seven years before.

"That isn't necessary, Daddy." She squeezed his hand reassuringly, then released it. "Chase can take care of me."

She extended her hand to Chase and met his gaze squarely. He hesitated only a split second before he stepped forward and clasped her hand in his own. Kneeling, he draped the hand she'd offered around his neck and gathered her up into his arms. Standing, he turned.

Kate's father stood in front of him, blocking his path to the front door. The man's face was blotched in anger, his lips pursed, his eyebrows gathered like thunderclouds over the bridge of his nose.

Chase tightened his grip on Kate. "Excuse me," he said in a voice that brooked no argument. "I'm taking Kate home." He shouldered his way past the man and headed for the front door with Kate's arms looped around his neck and her cheek pressed close to his.

When Kate's father would have followed them, Lilah McGinis placed a restraining hand on her husband's arm. "No, Jack."

He whipped his face around to stare at her, unaccustomed to anyone, much less his wife, getting in his way. She laced her arm through her husband's and smiled up at him. "Chase will take care of her."

He turned a worried face toward the path the crowd had made for Chase to pass through. "But she may need medical attention."

"She might, but I doubt it. Not yet, anyway." She smiled a secretive smile and squeezed her husband's arm to her side. "Better prepare yourself, dear," she said softly as she watched Chase and Kate disappear from sight. "Unless I miss my guess, I think you're going to be a grandfather again."

* * *

Kate's eyelashes fluttered as soft and feather-light as a butterfly's wings against his cheek. His cheeks were wet, but from Kate's tears or his own, he didn't know and didn't care. Ignoring the curious stares of the people milling about, he strode across the street and the vacant lot with Kate clutched tight his arms. He didn't stop until he reached his truck.

Resting the bulk of her weight on a raised knee, he freed one arm long enough to pull open the truck door, then maneuvered her onto the seat. When he would have released her, she clung to him.

"Hold me. Please."

The desperation in her voice ripped at his soul. He crawled onto the seat with her and pulled her onto his lap. He held her as sobs racked her slim shoulders, a wealth of emotion clogging his own throat. He wanted so badly to tell her that he loved her, that he needed her, and how much it had meant to him that she had turned to him and not to her father. But the words were lodged tight in his throat and wouldn't come.

Instead he held her, stroking her face, her hair, letting his hands say what he was incapable of putting into words. At last, she lifted her face to his. Their gazes met and she smiled. Gold flecks danced for him through a mist of tears.

"Take me home, Chase," she whispered as she lifted a hand to his cheek. "And make love with me."

The phone rang and Chase rolled to the side of the bed and grabbed it before it woke Kate. "Hello?" he said softly, so as not to disturb her.

"Morgan? That you?"

Chase immediately tensed at the sound of Jack McGinis's voice. "Yeah, it's me."

"How's Kate?"

Chase glanced across the width of bed. Kate lay where he'd left her, in a fetal curl, one hand tucked beneath her cheek. One bare shoulder peeked from beneath the crisp white sheet whose soft folds fell just short of covering a rose-colored nipple. Though he'd spent the last couple of hours satisfying a need that had raged within them both, desire pricked at his groin at the sight of her. "She's asleep."

"Good. She'll be needing all the rest she can get."

Chase frowned at the unusual comment, but chose not to pursue it.

"Kate tells me you're working on that historical preservation project downtown."

Chase didn't know why Jack McGinis was bringing up that particular subject, but he didn't trust the man any farther than he could throw him. "Yeah. What of it?"

"Just wanted to let you know, if you run into any trouble, you can call on me."

"Thanks," he said dryly. "But I can handle my own trouble."

A deep chuckle rumbled across the phone line. "I'm sure you can."

Chase thought he detected a hint of admiration in the simple comment, but rejected the notion. There was no love lost between the two men. "Do you want me to have Kate call you when she wakes up?"

"No, not unless she wants to. But you could do me one favor."

"Oh?" Chase asked suspiciously. "And what's that?"

"Marry the girl. Give my grandchild a good name."

Eleven

Grandchild! Chase's mouth sagged open. But before he could demand an explanation, he heard a click, then a dial tone.

"What the—?" He held out the receiver and stared at it, then slammed it down on its base.

"Who was that?" Kate asked, her voice groggy from sleep.

"Your father." Chase twisted around in the bed to look at her.

She pushed up on one elbow, auburn hair floating around her shoulders. The angry set of his jaw made her instantly alert. "Is something wrong?"

"He told me to marry you."

Kate's eyes widened. "He did?"

"Yeah. Said he wanted his *grandchild* to have a good name." Chase watched her face, waiting for her to laugh, to deny that she was pregnant with his child. She didn't. If possible, her eyes widened even more.

He rose from the bed and stalked across the room, both angered and hurt that she'd gone to her family with the news and not to him. "When were you going to tell me? Or were you going to let your father take care of this for you, too?" he asked, his voice damning her for her secrecy.

Kate jerked to a sitting position, gathering the sheets at her breasts in a tight fist. "Now just a darn minute. I didn't tell my father anything or ask him for anything, but to leave you alone."

"Then why did he say that?"

"I haven't a clue."

"*Are* you pregnant?"

Kate opened her mouth to deny the allegation, but slowly closed it. The fainting, the nausea. She felt the blood drain from her face. She lifted a limp hand and wiped at the beads of perspiration that had popped up on her forehead.

"Well, are you?" he demanded angrily.

"I don't know," she murmured, her mind whirling with the possibilities.

"You don't know!" he roared, then stalked back to the bed. He planted both hands on the mattress and leaned across to glare at her. "If *you* don't know, then who does?"

Kate placed trembling fingers at her temples as the fact that she might very well be pregnant gradually soaked in. "Will you please stop yelling at me?"

"I'll stop yelling when you tell me what the hell is going on!"

Grabbing a pillow and hugging it to her breasts, Kate scooted away from him until her back rested against the headboard. "I don't know if I'm pregnant or not, but I've been nauseated for about a week and fainted twice. What with all the stress of our relationship and the pressures associated with getting ready for the grand opening, I blamed the symptoms on that. I never thought…"

She lifted her face, her eyes flooded with tears. "I never used any protection, because I didn't think I could get pregnant. When I was married to Philip, my gynecologist told me I'd probably never have children. A tilted uterus, he said. One in a thousand chance of my ever conceiving." She swallowed hard as she realized that that number might very well have come up. "What are we going to do?"

The fear in her eyes had Chase crawling across the bed to gather her in his arms. "We're going to give this baby a name," he said.

Kate lifted her tear-stained face to look up at him, not believing what she'd just heard. "What did you say?"

He strained to peer over the side of the bed. "Can you reach my pants?"

Confused by the unexpected request, Kate frowned but reached over and nabbed his pants, then handed them to him. Holding the slacks in one hand, Chase held onto Kate with the other and scooted to a sitting position, pulling her to his lap.

"What are you doing?" she asked as he fished around in the pockets of his slacks.

"Looking for something."

"What?"

Change jingled in the right pocket as Chase switched to search the left, ignoring her. "In order to give the baby a name, we'll need to get married."

Kate's eyes widened, then narrowed, and her lips thinned to a tight line. She doubled up her fist and socked Chase in the stomach as hard as she could. He doubled over as the breath whooshed out of him.

She flounced off the bed, then wheeled to glare at him. "That has to be the most despicable proposal I've ever heard." She grabbed his shirt, started to pull it on, then threw it at him instead. "What happened to 'I love you and want to spend the rest of my life with you,' or are you incapable of such an emotional speech?" Kate stalked to her closet and yanked a robe off a hanger, then spun to glare at him again as she jerked it on.

Chase sat on the bed with the sheet draped low at his waist, trying hard not to grin. He pulled up his knees and draped his wrists to dangle loosely over them. He watched her storm around the room, knowing he'd made one hell of a mistake, but just as confident he could rectify it. "Are you through?" he asked quietly.

Kate refused to answer, but gave her head a defiant toss, sending tousled auburn hair flying.

Chase held out his hand. "Come here."

She looked at his hand, then back at him. "Uh-uh. If you want me, *you* come here."

He pushed back the sheet. "Okay, then meet me halfway."

Kate frowned as she watched him crawl to the end of the bed. He should have looked ridiculous—naked as the day he was born, knee following hand as he made his way across the length of the bed.

He didn't, which only infuriated her more.

He sat back on his heels and rested his palms on his knees. "Your turn."

"Last time we did this," she said, referring to their weekend at the cabin, "you cheated."

"No, I didn't. And, anyway, I've already moved my half of the distance."

Knowing he was right, Kate took a step, stopped, then

pushed her hands into fists at her sides and stomped to the foot of the bed. "What?"

He reached out and one by one uncurled her fingers from tight fists. When he'd done so, he looked her square in the eye. "I love you, Kate, and I want to spend the rest of my life with you."

Hearing her own words spouted back to her, she caught her lower lip between her teeth and ducked her head. "That's not a very original line."

He released one hand and tipped up her chin until she was forced to look at him.

"Will you marry me, Kate?"

Unable to meet the intensity of his blue eyes, Kate closed hers. A tear squeezed through her closed lids, hung precariously on her cheekbone for a second, then slid down her face.

Chase thumbed it away.

Her green eyes opened to meet his blue ones. "If it's just because I might be pregnant…" Her voice drifted off, unable to mention her deepest fears.

"No, that's not it. Whether you're pregnant or not, I love you, Kate, and want to marry you."

She sniffed, hearing his words, but not allowing herself to fully believe them. "You're just saying that because you know that's what I want you to say." She threw back her head and groaned her frustration at the ceiling before snapping her gaze back to his. "And why would you want to marry me, anyway? I have a horrible temper and I'm impulsive and stubborn."

"I know, but that's why I love you."

"It's all your fault," she said, wiping a wrist beneath her nose, acting as if she hadn't heard a word he'd said. "If you'd talk to me and tell me things, I wouldn't lose my temper. I never know what's going on in that head of yours."

Chase thought about that for a moment. "I've never been one much for talk. You can teach me."

"Okay," she agreed willingly. "You can start by telling me why you don't trust me."

He winced. How like Kate to cut straight to the heart of the matter. "I didn't, at first," he began slowly, knowing he had to be honest about his feelings. "I was scared to. I thought your coming back was like a seven year itch or something. I didn't know what you wanted or what you expected from me, and I wasn't about to commit myself until I knew." He dropped her hand and locked his arms around her waist, smiling up at her as he discovered it wasn't so hard to bare his soul.

"And now?" she persisted.

The memory of her letting go of her father's hand and reaching for his brought a lump of emotion to Chase's throat. "Love is built on trust, Kate. You don't have to prove anything to me anymore."

"Oh, Chase," she whispered, and threw her arms around his neck. He fell back on the bed, pulling her with him.

"Can you reach my pants?"

She propped her elbows on his chest and narrowed a frown at him. "Seems like this is where we started." She leaned across the bed and caught the discarded pants in her fingers.

"Now look in the pocket."

She stuck her hand in the right one.

"No. The other one."

She shifted her weight on Chase's chest and dipped into the left. Her finger caught on an object and she pulled it out. Her gaze settled on a ring.

But this was not just any ordinary ring. It was big—about

three inches in diameter—hinged with a tiny screw and made of heavy brass.

"What is *this?*" she asked, curling her nose in disgust.

Chase chuckled. "You don't know?"

Kate looked at him in exasperation. "Heavens, no! I've never seen anything like it in my life."

He took the ring from her and turned it around and around between his fingers. "It's a nose ring used on bulls." He held it above his lips, just short of his nose. "Ranchers put them through the bull's nostrils so they can lead them around, handle them easier. I bought this one," he said, holding up the ring for her inspection, "while I was in Austin. I thought you might need it."

Kate's forehead wrinkled in perplexity. "I don't understand."

"Well, I am sort of bullheaded," he said, chuckling. He sobered, then looked at her again. "Remember my offer to be the only bull in your pasture?"

Kate slowly nodded.

Chase handed her the ring. "The ring's yours to put in my nose whenever you're ready."

Kate closed her fingers around the cold metal. She glanced at Chase, then opened her hand and stared at the ring. Though she realized it was only a symbol and Chase never intended to really wear the grotesque thing, the meaning behind his gesture was all too clear. The only bull in the pasture, huh?

She sniffed again. Then she snorted. Then she laughed as she leaned across his chest and lightly touched the ring to the end of his nose.

"I'm ready."

"Me, too," he murmured as he took the ring from her hand

and tossed it across the room. "But first I'd like to scratch that itch just one more time, just to be sure." He planted his lips on hers and rolled, pinning Kate, laughing, beneath him.

* * * * *

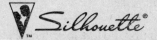

Silhouette®

Romantic
SUSPENSE

**Sparked by Danger,
Fueled by Passion.**

Mission: Impassioned

A brand-new miniseries begins with

My Spy

By *USA TODAY* bestselling author

Marie Ferrarella

She had to trust him with her life....
It was the most daring mission of Joshua Lazlo's
career: rescuing the prime minister of England's
daughter from a gang of cold-blooded kidnappers.
But nothing prepared the shadowy secret agent
for a fiery woman whose touch ignited something
far more dangerous.

My Spy

#1472

Available July 2007 wherever you buy books!

Visit Silhouette Books at www.eHarlequin.com   SRS27542

REQUEST YOUR FREE BOOKS!
2 FREE NOVELS PLUS 2 FREE GIFTS!

Silhouette®

SPECIAL EDITION®
Life, Love and Family!

YES! Please send me 2 FREE Silhouette Special Edition® novels and my 2 FREE gifts. After receiving them, if I don't wish to receive any more books, I can return the shipping statement marked "cancel." If I don't cancel, I will receive 6 brand-new novels every month and be billed just $4.24 per book in the U.S., or $4.99 per book in Canada, plus 25¢ shipping and handling per book and applicable taxes, if any*. That's a savings of at least 15% off the cover price! I understand that accepting the 2 free books and gifts places me under no obligation to buy anything. I can always return a shipment and cancel at any time. Even if I never buy another book from Silhouette, the two free books and gifts are mine to keep forever.

235 SDN EEYU 335 SDN EEY6

Name	(PLEASE PRINT)	
Address		Apt.
City	State/Prov.	Zip/Postal Code

Signature (if under 18, a parent or guardian must sign)

Mail to the Silhouette Reader Service™:
IN U.S.A.: P.O. Box 1867, Buffalo, NY 14240-1867
IN CANADA: P.O. Box 609, Fort Erie, Ontario L2A 5X3

Not valid to current Silhouette Special Edition subscribers.

Want to try two free books from another line?
Call 1-800-873-8635 or visit www.morefreebooks.com.

* Terms and prices subject to change without notice. NY residents add applicable sales tax. Canadian residents will be charged applicable provincial taxes and GST. This offer is limited to one order per household. All orders subject to approval. Credit or debit balances in a customer's account(s) may be offset by any other outstanding balance owed by or to the customer. Please allow 4 to 6 weeks for delivery.

Your Privacy: Silhouette is committed to protecting your privacy. Our Privacy Policy is available online at www.eHarlequin.com or upon request from the Reader Service. From time to time we make our lists of customers available to reputable firms who may have a product or service of interest to you. If you would prefer we not share your name and address, please check here. ☐

SSE07

Silhouette®

Desire

THE GARRISONS
A brand-new family saga begins with

THE CEO'S SCANDALOUS AFFAIR
BY ROXANNE ST. CLAIRE

Eldest son Parker Garrison is preoccupied running
his Miami hotel empire and dealing with his recently
deceased father's secret second family. Since he has
little time to date, taking his superefficient assistant
to a charity event should have been a simple plan.
Until passion takes them beyond business.

Don't miss any of the six exciting titles in
THE GARRISONS continuity, beginning in July.
Only from Silhouette Desire.

THE CEO'S SCANDALOUS AFFAIR
#1807

Available July 2007.